THE GUNSMITH GETS THIRSTY

mayor?"

"How did you know that?"

"Two gringos in town in two days. Will you try to break him out of jail before he can be hung for his crime?"

"That would be against the law."

"*Sí*, señor," the man said, "and we are all deputies. If you tried to help your friend we would be forced to shoot you."

Clint looked around and saw that the other men in the cantina all had pistols stuck into their belts.

"I get the point," he said.

"*Bueno,*" the bartender said, "that is very good, señor. Would you like another beer? How do you say, on the house?"

"Yes," Clint said. "And I'll buy one for everyone else in here."

In seconds Clint was the most popular man in the town of Two Beers. But he knew that wasn't going to help him break Pete out of jail. He'd have to buy the whole town a whole lot of beers so they'd be too drunk to shoot straight—and then somebody was liable to hit one of them by accident, anyway.

DON'T MISS THESE
ALL-ACTION WESTERN SERIES
FROM THE BERKLEY PUBLISHING GROUP

THE GUNSMITH

210

MAXIMILIAN'S TREASURE

J. R. ROBERTS

JOVE BOOKS, NEW YORK

MAXIMILIAN'S TREASURE

A Jove Book / published by arrangement with
the author

PRINTING HISTORY
Jove edition / July 1999

The Penguin Putnam Inc. World Wide Web site address is
http://www.penguinputnam.com

ISBN: 0-515-12534-2

A JOVE BOOK®
Jove Books are published by The Berkley Publishing Group,
a division of Penguin Putnam Inc.,
375 Hudson Street, New York, New York 10014.
JOVE and the "J" design
are trademarks belonging to Penguin Putnam Inc.

PRINTED IN THE UNITED STATES OF AMERICA

10 9 8 7 6 5 4 3 2 1

ONE

Dos Cervezas was a small town just across the Rio Grande from Texas. Like most border towns, it was small and lazy, something Clint Adams thought he could appreciate at the moment. He'd been to too many busy towns of late, and was looking forward to some peace and quiet.

Although, if that was what he was really looking for, then why was he coming here to meet his friend Pete Townsend? Every time he got involved with Townsend, he ended up with people shooting at him—*lots* of people shooting at him.

Or so it seemed.

He shook his head and laughed. Pete Townsend had to be a real likable guy because even with that history Clint still liked him and still responded to a telegram asking him to meet Pete in the small Mexican border town called Two Beers.

Clint stopped at the small livery, took one look at the old, rheumy-eyed liveryman sitting by the door and said, "That's all right, Papa, don't trouble yourself. I'll take care of my horse myself."

The old man nodded, waved, and settled back into his chair.

1

Clint unsaddled the big black gelding, rubbed him down and fed him, then left him with the promise to return that night to make sure he was all right. Duke gave him a baleful stare and then went about eating his fill.

There was only one hotel in Two Beers. This he had learned from Pete Townsend's telegram. It said, "Meet me at the Hotel Grande in a town called Dos Cervezas."

The Hotel Grande was anything but. Clint entered and had to wake the clerk to get a room.

"I'm looking for a friend."

"Friend, señor?"

"Friend," Clint said, and then added, "Amigo."

"And this amigo?" the clerk asked. "His name would be?"

"You speak English."

The clerk grinned—although it was anything but a friendly grin—and said, "And very well, too, señor. You have a room and you want a friend. Does the señor wish a woman, as well?"

"No," Clint said, "right now I'm just looking for my friend, Pete Townsend."

"Ah," the clerk said, nodding his head. "Señor Townsend."

"You know him, then?"

"Sí, señor," the clerk said, "everyone in town knows Mr. Townsend."

"Really? And why is that?"

"Because, señor," the clerk said. "He is to be hanged in three days."

After Clint got over his shock, he asked the clerk where Townsend was now.

"Where else, señor?" the man asked. "He is in jail."

"And did he have a trial?"

"Oh, sí," the clerk said, "he had a trial, señor, all legal."

"And what's he accused of?"

"He is *convicted* of killing our illustrious mayor," the clerk said, "when the mayor caught him with his daughter, señor."

"Sure," Clint said, half to himself, "there had to be a daughter involved."

"Oh, *sí*, señor," the clerk said. "Carmalita, the mayor's virginal daughter. That is, she *was* a virgin."

"She was, huh?"

The clerk simply shrugged.

"And when did this happen?"

"Yesterday, señor."

"And there was a trial already?"

"*Sí*, señor," the man said. "Yesterday. The whole town was there."

"And did my friend have a lawyer?"

"Your friend defended himself, señor."

Well, Townsend wasn't a lawyer, but he did have the gift of gab. It worked with women, but apparently not with a jury—or judge, whichever he'd had.

"Well, thanks for the information," Clint said. "I'll take my gear up to my room."

"Won't you be going to see your friend, señor?" the man asked.

"Soon," Clint said. "If he's locked up, he won't be going anywhere, will he?"

"No, señor," the clerk said, "not for three days, and then he goes to meet his Maker."

Clint went up to his room, dropped his saddlebags onto the hard bed, and leaned his rifle against the wall in the corner. He walked to the window and looked down at the street. He didn't hear the sound of a gallows being built, so he assumed they were going to hang his friend from a beam in the livery, or from a nearby tree.

Not if he could help it, though.

TWO

The sheriff—*el jefe*—looked up from the apple he was methodically peeling with a Kentucky toothpick Clint thought he recognized.

"Sheriff?"

"I am Sheriff Ignacio Perez," the fat man said. "What can I do for you, señor?"

"I understand you have a friend of mine here."

"Do I, señor?"

"I don't know," Clint said, "do you?"

The man finished the row of peel he was working on and stopped when it dropped to the desktop.

"What is your friend's name, señor?"

"Townsend, Peter Townsend."

"Ah, *sí*," the sheriff said, "Señor Townsend is my guest."

"Your guest?"

The sheriff shrugged and said, "Prisoner has such a . . . nasty sound to it."

He started on another row of apple peel. Clint had seen Pete Townsend use that very same knife to peel an apple in one continuous row.

"Can I see him?"

The sheriff, a tremendously fat man, did not look up

5

from his peel as he said, "He is in the back, señor. You cannot miss him. I only have one cell, and he is in it."

The sheriff seemed to find this very funny and started to laugh, and stopped when his own laughter caused him to cut the peel short.

"Caramba!" he swore.

"You need to concentrate a little more," Clint said, and walked into the back room that housed the one cell.

"Clint? Is that you?"

"Who else would it be?" Clint replied.

His friend got up from the cot he'd been lying on and came to the front of the cell.

"You gotta get me out of here!" he said. "These crazy Mexicans are gonna hang me."

"For deflowering the mayor's daughter?" Clint asked. "Or for killing him?"

"I didn't deflower nobody," Townsend said. "That gal was deflowered a long time ago."

"But you did kill the mayor?"

"He tried to shoot me! I had to defend myself."

"Pete," Clint asked, "when did you get here?"

"Yesterday."

"And you couldn't stay out of trouble for one day until I got here?"

"Clint," Townsend said, "wait until you see this girl. Thick black hair, black eyes, and great big—"

"Never mind," Clint said. "I've got to figure out a way to get you out of here before they string you up."

"Just . . . get me out."

"How?"

"Go get the keys," Townsend said. "You think that fat sheriff is gonna stop you?"

"He locked you up, didn't he? And took your knife?"

"He's using my knife?"

"To peel an apple."

"Son of a bitch," Townsend said. "Yeah, he locked me up. What was I gonna do, shoot a lawman?"

"But you want me to?"

"Naw, I don't want you to shoot him," Townsend said. "Just scare him."

"How?"

"Tell him who you are. That scares people."

Clint studied his friend. It had been a couple of years since he'd seen him, but he looked the same—ten years younger than he was, a healthy, robust man who attracted women like honey attracted flies.

"That curly brown hair's starting to get a little thin, isn't it?" Clint asked.

"What?" Townsend's hand went to his head. "It is not!"

"Pete," Clint said, "I'm not going to scare the sheriff into letting you go. Where's the judge who tried you?"

"Tried me?" Townsend said. "You call that a trial? It was a travesty of justice, that's what it was."

"Maybe it was the closest thing to justice they have in this town. Who was the judge?"

"Well, the mayor was the judge, but since he was dead the sheriff acted as judge."

"Well, that's not legal."

"What do these people care about legal? They want to hang a gringo."

"Let me think," Clint said. "If this thing isn't legal, I won't have any qualms about breaking you out."

"Fine," Townsend said, "do it."

"But are you planning to stay in Mexico or head back across the border?"

"We're staying in Mexico!" Townsend said. "I got something to show you you're not gonna believe."

"Well, if we're going to stay in this country we don't want the *rurales* on our trail, do we?"

"There won't be no *rurales*," Townsend said, "and no posse. That sheriff ain't about to try and get on a horse."

"You're sure of that?"

"Christ, Clint," Townsend said, "you've *seen* him."

"Yeah, you might be right," Clint said. "Okay, I'll see what I can do. I'll be back."

"Back? Get me out of here *now*. The food might kill me before they can hang me!"

"Relax, Pete," Clint said. "I just have to figure something out, is all. I'll be back soon."

"Don't leave me here. Clint—"

Clint left, figuring a little time in a Mexican cell might do his friend some good.

THREE

The sheriff still hadn't finished peeling the apple when Clint returned to the man's desk. Clint hoped that, for his own sake, the man wasn't going to try to core it.

"Sheriff?"

"*Sí*, señor."

"I understand you were the judge who tried my friend."

"He killed the only judge we had," the sheriff said. "Someone had to do it."

"Do you intend to turn him over to the *rurales*?" Clint asked.

The knife almost went through the man's palm at the word *rurales*. He put the knife down and looked up at Clint with frightened eyes. In spite of what he had told Pete Townsend, it looked like he had succeeded in scaring the sheriff.

"We do not like to have the *rurales* come around here, señor," the sheriff said. "No, I do not intend to turn him over. We tried him, and we will execute him here."

"You tried him so quickly, why put the execution off for three days?" Clint asked.

9

The sheriff spread his fat hands and said, "Everyone wants to be there, señor."

"I see."

"You, uh, don't intend to try to stop us, do you, señor?"

"I guess that depends, Sheriff."

"On what, señor?"

"On how many deputies you have."

"I have deputized the whole town for this, señor," the sheriff said.

"Why did you do that, Sheriff?"

"So that if the prisoner tries to escape anyone can shoot him."

"Now he's a prisoner?" Clint asked. "What happened to guest?"

"How do you say it in your country, señor?" the sheriff asked. "You call a spade a spade?"

"You've been to my country, Sheriff?"

"In my youth."

The sheriff seemed to have gotten over his fright and picked up the knife and the apple again.

"Is there anything else I can do for you, señor?"

Clint knew he could have taken Townsend out of there right then, if he wanted to, but he wanted to take a good look around town first. He wanted to see how many of these "deputies" were actually armed.

"No, Sheriff," Clint said. "Not right now. You've been very helpful already."

"Then I bid you good day, señor," the lawman said.

"Good day."

When Clint left, the sheriff was staring at the apple and frowning, as if he'd lost his place and couldn't find it again.

Clint took a short walk around the lazy town of Two Beers. It was all he needed to see that the people who lived here took their civic duty seriously. All of the men he saw were armed, and at one point he saw a woman putting a revolver into the pocket of her dress. If he'd tried to take Townsend out of the jail they would have been shot down in seconds.

He needed a plan.

And something to eat.

He found a small café and went inside. There were about eight tables, and they were all empty at this hour. Something was cooking, though, because the smells coming from the kitchen made his mouth water. The one thing Clint really liked about Mexico—besides the women— was the food. He waited a few moments, then scuffed his feet for a while until somebody noticed and came out of the kitchen.

The woman who appeared was in her forties. She was full and firmly built, with large breasts that were shown off by a low-cut peasant blouse, and shapely legs. Perhaps her waist wasn't as slender as it had been when she was a girl, but Clint certainly didn't hold that against her. She had long, black hair and a pleasant face that was perhaps a little too firm of jaw. All in all a handsome woman.

"Señor, you wish to eat?"

"Please."

"You may take any table," she said, and he took one that was in a corner. If she thought this odd she didn't comment.

"I have some enchiladas, some tacos, some rice. Or would you like something else? Perhaps . . . a steak?"

"No, thank you, señorita."

"Señora," she said, "although my husband is . . . quite dead."

"Señora, whatever you have cooking in the kitchen that is sending out those wonderful smells will be fine with me."

"Muy bien," she said. "I will bring it out to you . . . and to drink?"

"In this town?" he asked. "What else but *cerveza*?"

She smiled and repeated, "What else?"

FOUR

Clint ate with gusto. The food was bursting with flavor and when he asked for more the waitress responded with great satisfaction.

"Another beer," she said, bringing him a second mug, filled to the brim. "It is—how do you gringos say—on the house?"

"Thank you, Carmen." She had introduced herself when she brought him her food. When he responded with his name she showed no signs of recognition.

When he finished eating there was still no one else in the café.

"Your food is delicious," he said.

"*Gracias.* I prepare it myself."

"Why are there no other customers? Don't they know how good it is?"

"Ah, they are staying away out of respect," she said, waving a hand to indicate that she did not feel the same respect, herself.

"Respect for who?"

"My husband."

"I thought you said your husband was dead?"

"He is," she said. "He was killed yesterday. He was the owner of this café."

13

"Your husband . . . was killed yesterday?"

"*Sí.*"

"Was he also . . . the mayor of this town?"

"Ah, I see you have already heard the story. *Sí.* Esteban Morales was the mayor, and he was my husband."

For the moment he put off telling her how he had heard the story.

"Forgive me if I'm speaking out of turn, Carmen, but you don't seem to be too upset about your husband being killed."

"I am not," she said. "He was a pig, and now that he is dead the people of this town revere him as a saint. Now, my first husband, there was a man."

"What happened to him?"

"He also died."

"How?"

"I caught him with another woman," she said. "He was too much man for only one."

"And what happened?"

She shrugged and said, "I shot him. I would have shot Esteban, too—my second husband, the mayor—but you don't shoot a man for being a pig, only for being a cheater."

"I see."

"So they are staying away because now that he is dead they think they respected him. The dead always command respect, have you noticed that?"

"I have, yes."

"The gringo who killed my husband," she said suddenly. "Is he a friend of yours?"

He hesitated, then answered, "Yes, how did you know?"

"Two gringos in town in two days is too much to be a coincidence," she said. "Did you hear what happened?"

"Only that your husband tried to shoot him for deflowering your daughter and my friend shot him in self-defense.''

She sat opposite him and leaned her arms on the table so that her breasts almost spilled out of her blouse.

"First," she said, "she was his daughter, not mine. Second, she was deflowered a long time ago, so there was no danger of your friend doing that."

"That's what he said."

"And he was right."

"Did you say this at the trial?"

She made a rude sound with her mouth that he found sexy and said, "Trial! That was no trial. They did not call any witnesses. They knew they were going to find him guilty and sentence him to hang before they even started."

"So they wouldn't let you testify?"

"They would not listen to anything I said," she told him. "Suddenly their beloved mayor was a saint and I was a—well, a *puta* for kicking him out of my bed."

"They knew that?"

"The whole town knew it."

"Tell me what you know about the sheriff."

She made that sound again. He liked the way she puckered her full lips when she did it. He thought she knew that he liked it.

"Another pig," she said. "A fat pig who does not want to leave his desk, so he comes up with the idea of deputizing the whole town."

"Does that mean you're a deputy?"

She frowned, then said, "I suppose it does."

That gave Clint an idea, but he wasn't ready to present it yet.

"Carmen, is there any question that your husband's daughter and my friend were together?"

"None," she said. "She crawled into his bed the moment he got here. He was her type, you know."

"He's most women's type."

"Not mine," she said, looking him right in the eye so that he got the message.

"Could you bring me to her so I could talk to her?"

"It will do no good," Carmen said. "She will try to get you into bed, and she might succeed. She is very beautiful."

"As beautiful as you?" he asked.

"Well," she said, with a slow smile, "perhaps not *that* beautiful."

FIVE

The similarities in the name had led Clint to believe that Carmen was Carmalita's mother.

"That is all we have in common," Carmen said, and when he met the younger girl Clint had to disagree. The other thing they both had in common was that raw sexuality that reached out and grabbed a man by the . . . throat.

Carmen arranged for Clint to meet Carmalita.

"What did you tell her?" he asked.

"The truth," she said. "That you are friends with the gringo who killed her father."

They were speaking outside the café after Carmen had closed for the day. Clint had occupied himself during the day by sitting in front of the hotel and counting the number of times the same people passed him by. He saw one man six different times.

"Come," Carmen said, "she is waiting."

She took him to the house she had shared with her husband and with Carmalita; the young woman was there, waiting on the porch. It was as they approached— even before he was close enough to make out her features—that he felt the impact of her beauty.

"I lied," Carmen said as they approached the house.

17

"About what?"

"She is more beautiful than I am," the older woman said. "Even I can see that."

Clint chose not to say anything to that.

"Carmalita," Carmen said, as they stepped up onto the porch of the remarkably well-kept house, "this is Clint Adams."

"Pete's friend," Carmalita said.

"Yes."

She and Carmen had the same black hair, but while Carmen's was wavy, Carmalita's was perfectly straight, parted down the center, and hung down to her waist.

"I am going inside," Carmen said, "so the two of you can talk."

"I will prepare dinner, Mama dear," Carmalita said. Clint noticed that Carmen hunched her shoulders slightly when the girl called her "Mama." She went into the house without another word.

"She hates when I call her 'Mama,' " Carmalita said to Clint.

"Then why do you do it?"

She looked at him, frowning as if he were stupid, and said, "Because she hates it."

"I see."

"Would you like to sit, Señor Adams?" she asked. "It will take a long time if you are going to convince me to change my story to save Pete."

"And why is that, Carmalita?" he asked, ignoring the chairs on the porch.

"Well," she said, "for one thing I would look very foolish if I did."

"And for another?"

"I got what I wanted out of this," she said.

"Which is?"

"My father is dead."

"Did you hate your father that much?"

She frowned again. He found that it was the only time she did not look utterly beautiful.

"I did not hate him at all."

"Then why are you glad he's dead?"

"Because now I am free," she said. "Free to leave this place."

"And he wouldn't let you leave?"

"Never!"

"And you don't hate him for that?"

"No," she said, "he was just . . . in my way . . . holding me back. Now I can go."

"Where?"

"To your country."

"Why did you pick Pete to kill your father?"

"I had tried with others," she said, "but they ran from my father's anger. Pete did not."

"I see," Clint said. "It just worked out that way, that Pete was the one who wasn't afraid."

She stood with her hands behind her back, her breasts thrust forward. They were not as large as Carmen's, but they were perfect, firm and round. She, too, wore a peasant blouse but it was pulled up higher so that her cleavage did not show. She didn't need it, really.

"I like Pete," she said, "I really do, but I can't help him."

"Why not?"

"Because it would make me look foolish."

"Your father tried to kill him," Clint said, "because he thought Pete had taken your virtue. I get the feeling that your father was the only one in town who thought you still *had* your virtue. Doesn't that make you feel foolish?"

"No," she said, "it makes my father seem foolish. Once he has been dead a while and people stop revering him, they will see this."

She had large eyes, black eyes, as Pete had said. Clint could see why Pete had been drawn to her, why he couldn't even stay out of trouble one day with this girl in the same town with him.

"So you won't change your story in any way to help Pete?"

"How can I change it?" she asked. "And not come out as a liar the first time?"

"I don't know."

"Perhaps you will stay to dine with us and we can discuss it?" she asked. "We could get Mama to leave us alone."

He didn't know how she had done it, because he hadn't noticed a particular movement, but suddenly her blouse was down enough to reveal her cleavage.

"No," he said, firmly.

"No . . . what?"

"No, I don't think I should be alone with you."

"You do not trust yourself?" she asked with a sly smile.

"Oh, yes," he said, "I always trust *myself*."

SIX

As he went inside, Carmalita stepped off the porch and walked away from the house. He found Carmen in the kitchen, cooking.

"She left," he said. "I guess you have to cook."

"She does not cook," Carmen said, "ever."

"Why did she say—"

"It is a game she plays," Carmen said, "like calling me 'Mama.'" She turned and looked at him over her shoulder. The big black eyes could have been Carmalita's, but the wavy black hair, that was all Carmen. "Did it help?"

"Did what help?"

"Talking to her?"

"No, it didn't."

"Did she try to get you alone?"

"Yes."

"You resisted."

"Yes."

"Why?"

"I have my mind on someone else."

"Your friend?"

"No."

She turned her attention back to what she was doing,

which was chopping vegetables. He sensed that she was pleased with his answer.

"Do you see now why your friend could not resist her?" she asked.

"Yes," Clint said, "but he's younger than I am."

Carmen pointed out, "That kind of beauty has no age."

"Looking at you I can believe it."

She stopped chopping then, turned around, and leaned back against the counter. Her large breasts strained the fabric of her blouse, and he could see her nipples clearly outlined.

"I would like to make love with you, now, on the kitchen floor."

He swallowed.

"But my husband died yesterday, do you understand? I did not love him, and I do not mourn him, but . . ."

"I understand, Carmen," he said.

"Do you want me, too?"

"Yes."

She moved close to him, pressed her breasts against his chest, and kissed him. Her tongue slithered into his mouth, her lips mashed up against his; he could smell the cooking odors in her hair, feel her hands on his back and neck. She broke the kiss and stepped away. Her eyes were moist, her breath came quickly.

"A promise," she said breathlessly, "of more to come. That is all I can give you right now."

He cleared his throat and said, "I guess it will have to be enough . . . for now."

"You will stay to eat?"

"No," he said, "I better go."

There was just too much womanhood in that house for him to stay.

"Come to the café tomorrow morning," she said, "for breakfast. I will make you *huevos rancheros*."

"I'll be there, Carmen."

They stared at each other for a few long moments and then she said, "You better go."

"Yes," he agreed, "I better."

He turned, left the kitchen and walked out of the house. His erection was painfully full and he stood still on the porch for a few moments until he felt it was safe to walk back to town.

He walked back to the hotel, for want of something better to do. The clerk was dozing at the desk. He started past him, then backtracked and woke the man up.

"Huh? Wha—"

"Are you a deputy?"

"What?"

"I asked if you are a deputy."

"I—uh, *sí*, yes, I am deputized by the sheriff. We all are."

"Do you have a gun?"

"Of course."

The man took an ancient-looking Walker Colt from beneath the desk. It was huge, and Clint doubted that the clerk could hit anything with it.

"I see," Clint said. "Thanks. You can go back to sleep now."

The man frowned, returned the Colt to its place beneath the desk, then sat back, folded his arms, and resumed his siesta.

Clint went up to his room, unlocked the door, and stepped inside. Carmalita was on his bed, the sheet tossed carelessly to the floor. She was lying on her back, completely naked, and as he entered she arched her back and stretched.

SEVEN

Clint's mouth was dry. There was no doubt that this young woman was possibly the most beautiful, desirable thing he'd ever seen. There was also no doubt that he didn't want to sleep with her. He would have preferred to find Carmen in his bed, if he hadn't just left her at her small house.

"Carmalita . . ."

"You want me," she said, as if hypnotizing him. "I can always tell when a man wants me."

He laughed and said, "That's because all men want you."

"Yes."

She sat up and he took in the sight of her round, firm breasts, the dark nipples, her long, smooth legs. Her hair was hanging down past her shoulders, like a see-through curtain on her breasts.

"Come to bed," she said.

"No."

She leaned back on her hands, which caused her breasts to thrust forward, and then she slid her legs open for him. He could see the pink slit through the curly black hair, see that she was already wet. In fact, he could *smell* her readiness—and his reaction, his *need*, was

25

pushing against the front of his pants, but he had no intention of giving in.

"Get up, Carmalita," he said, "and get dressed." He started looking for her clothes.

"I threw them out the window," she said.

"What?"

"My clothes," she said. "I threw them out the window."

He hadn't seen any clothes down on the street. Could they have gotten caught somewhere? Or was she lying?

"I don't believe you," he said.

"Why not?"

"Because women don't treat their clothes that way."

"They are just clothes." She opened and closed her legs, wriggling her toes and keeping her eyes on them as she did it.

"Then they're under the bed."

She smiled and said, "You'll have to come close to the bed to find out."

He had no intentions of getting close to that bed. While he kept his distance he thought he could resist her. After all, he wasn't Pete Townsend.

"Are you afraid of me?" she taunted.

"No."

"There is no papa to come in and shoot you."

"I know that."

"I am not a virgin."

"I know that, too."

"Even before your amigo, I was not a virgin."

"I know that, too."

"Come," she said, lifting her arms to him, looking at him now. The movement made her breasts lift as well, pointing the hard nipples at him. "You want me."

"No," he said, "I don't."

"You must."

She had moved his saddlebags over to a chair so she could get into bed. Behind the chair was his rifle, leaning against the wall. He took two steps, grabbed the saddle-bags and the rifle.

"What are you doing?" she asked.

"Getting another room," he said. "You can stay in this one."

"You are running away from me."

"Yes," he said, opening the door.

"Because you want me!"

"If I wanted you," he said, "I wouldn't be running."

Suddenly, as he closed the door behind him, he heard her calling him names, but they were in Spanish. He thought he heard *cabrone*, but couldn't make out any others.

Now he hoped she *had* thrown her clothes out the window.

When he got downstairs the clerk was smiling at him.

"There's a girl in my room."

"Si, señor," the man said, "and what a girl."

"I want another room."

"Two rooms, señor?" the man asked. "Will there be two girls?"

"I want one room," Clint said, "and no girls, understand?"

"No girls?"

"None," Clint said. "Don't let any girls into my room. Understand?"

"*Si*, señor," the man said, and then added, "no, señor—"

"Never mind," Clint said. "Just give me another—a different room."

The clerk looked up the stairs, as if he expected to see Carmalita coming down any moment.

"Is she still upstairs, señor?"

"Yes."

"In your room?"

"In what was my room," Clint said. "You're going to give me a new room."

"But . . . why, señor?"

"Because," Clint said, very patiently, "the last man who slept with that girl is going to be hanged in three days. Is that a good enough reason for you?"

"That is an excellent reason, señor," the man said, and gave Clint the key to a different room.

EIGHT

Clint went to his new room and left his rifle and saddle-bags there. It was at the farthest end of the hall from the room Carmalita was in and the only window overlooked the alley. He decided not to stay in the hotel, because the girl just might come down the hall naked and start pounding on his door. It wasn't that he thought she wanted him that much, he just thought she wasn't used to being turned down by men.

He left the hotel and found his way to the nearest saloon, or cantina, as they called them here. There were several men seated at tables, but the bar was empty. He chose to stand at the bar.

"Beer," he told the bartender.

"*Sí*, señor."

The bartender went and got the beer and brought it back to him, then stayed and asked, "You are friends with the gringo who shot our mayor?"

"How did you know that?"

The man shrugged beefy shoulders and said, "Two gringos in town in two days . . ."

Well then, there it was. It was no secret that he and Townsend were friends. That was going to make it all the more difficult for him to get his friend out of jail.

"Will you try to break him out of jail before he can be hanged for his crime?"

"That would be against the law."

"*Sí*, señor," the man said, "and we are all deputies. If you tried to help your friend we would be forced to shoot you."

"Is that a fact?"

"*Sí* señor, it is."

Clint looked around and saw the other men in the cantina looking at him. They all had pistols stuck into their belts. There was not a holster among them. When he looked back the bartender was also holding a pistol.

"I get the point," he said.

"You will not try anything?" the bartender asked. "We would hate to have to kill you, señor."

"I would be foolish to try anything, wouldn't I?"

"*Sí*, señor, but it is our experience that gringos are very foolish people."

From behind him Clint heard a man mutter, "Crazy gringos."

"You're right," Clint said, "some of them are foolish, but not me."

"*Bueno*," the bartender said, putting his gun back beneath the bar, "that is very good, señor. Would you like another beer? How do you say, on the house?"

"Yes," Clint said, "I would like another beer on the house . . . and I'll buy one for everyone else in here."

In seconds he was the most popular man in the town of Two Beers.

When Clint left the cantina he knew that buying half a dozen men beer wasn't going to help him break Townsend out of jail. He'd have to buy the whole town a whole lot of beers so they'd be too drunk to shoot straight—and somebody was liable to hit one of them by accident, anyway.

He walked back to his hotel and stopped in front to

see if any women's clothes were on the ground, or if they'd gotten caught on anything. Satisfied that there were none to be seen, he went inside.

"Did you see the girl leave?" he asked the clerk.

"*Sí*, señor."

"Was she . . . dressed?"

"*Sí*, señor."

"Did she ask for my room number?"

"*S-sí*, señor."

"Did you give it to her?"

"*S-s-sí*, señor, but I could not help it."

Clint stared at the man, then said, "No, I guess you couldn't. You didn't let her into the room, did you?"

"Oh, no, señor."

Probably because she hadn't asked this time, Clint thought. Carmalita probably had to go home and figure out what to do now that a man had turned her down.

"I'm going to my room now," Clint said. "Don't send *any* women up, understand?"

"Yes, sir."

"In fact, if anyone asks, I'm not here."

"*Sí*, señor."

"If my sleep is disturbed," Clint said, "I'm going to come down here and disturb you. Do you understand?"

"P-perfectly, señor."

"Tell me something," Clint continued.

"Anything, señor."

"Why does everyone in this town speak such good English?"

"The border, señor," the man said. "We are close to the border."

That made sense. In fact, Clint felt stupid for even asking the question. Obviously, he needed some sleep.

"What's your name?"

"Ramon, señor."

"Well, good night, Ramon."

"Good night, señor."

Clint went up to his new room, slipped the key into the lock, and opened the door quickly. He was happy to find that it—and the bed—were empty.

He laid down on the thin mattress, doubted he'd be able to fall asleep on the thing, and in minutes did.

NINE

When Clint rose the next morning he realized he had two days to save Pete Townsend from the gallows. It was a big responsibility, one he should be taking more seriously. There was no point in making poor Pete wait until the last minute.

From the accounts he had heard, it certainly sounded like self-defense to him, but this was Mexico. He knew that if they were in the United States, he'd be able to get his friend a fair trial. That wasn't the case here. As far as these people were concerned, Townsend had been tried and convicted and all that remained was for the sentence to be carried out.

He'd seen enough of the "deputized" people in town to know that they could end up being shot by accident. If he was going to take Townsend out of there, it definitely could not be out in the open. That meant he probably couldn't do it in the daytime. He was going to have to plan a nighttime jailbreak.

If he went to the livery and took Townsend's horse out, word might get to the sheriff, or to some of the deputies, so even that was going to have to be done at night.

He decided to first go to the livery and identify Townsend's horse.

When he reached the stable, the same old man was sitting in his chair, dozing. Since Clint was walking instead of riding he was able to slip past the man without waking him up. Inside he checked all the stalls. He hadn't seen Townsend in a couple of years, but if the man was riding the same horse he'd recognize it. Sure enough, he found it in a back stall, right next to Duke. It was a little roan that Townsend had become real partial to. Just to be sure, he also checked the saddle and recognized that, as well.

So now he had the horse spotted. What he needed now was to find out how long the old man kept the livery open and if, when it wasn't open, whether it was actually locked. In a town this small it was possible that it wasn't.

He left the livery, still without waking the old man, and went to the jail.

The fat sheriff was still seated at his desk; when Clint asked to see Townsend, the man just waved at him.

"You come to get me out?" Townsend demanded as soon as he saw Clint.

"One way or another," Clint said, "I'm going to get you out of here."

"Well, I'm glad to hear that," his friend replied, "but why can't you just take me out of here now?"

"Because this whole town is armed, that's why." Clint went on to explain that the sheriff had deputized every citizen in town.

"How are we gonna get out of here, then?"

Clint waved at Townsend to lower his voice.

"We'll do it at night," he said. "I'll bring your horse around back and we'll go out that way. Does the sheriff sleep here in the jail?"

"I guess so," Townsend said. "I never hear him

leave, and at night I can hear the fat bastard breathing hard.''

"Okay," Clint said, "you've got to understand one thing, Pete."

"What's that?"

"I want to take you out of here without hurting anyone, without shooting anyone."

"I never wanted to hurt or shoot anyone in the first place," Townsend said. "That old man just busted in on us waving a gun. I didn't have a choice."

"Sure you did," Clint said. "You could have stayed away from that girl."

"Have you seen her yet?" Townsend asked. "Could *you* stay away from her?"

"As a matter if fact, yes, I could, and I have," Clint said. "She showed up in my room, naked in my bed."

Townsend's eyes popped.

"And you turned her down?"

"I changed rooms," Clint said. "I *ran* out of there, Pete, and that's what you should have done."

Townsend shook his head. "You're a better man than me if you can resist her, Clint."

"Well, let's forget who the better man is. I don't know if it's going to be tonight or tomorrow night, Pete, but just be ready to get out of here at a moment's notice."

"I'm ready now!" Townsend said.

"I know you are, but I don't want us getting shot by accident," Clint said. "I don't know about you, but I don't want to die that way, shot by mistake by some storekeeper."

"It'd be better than hanging," Townsend said.

"You're probably right about that," Clint said. It was probably unfair to expect Townsend, who was staring at a rope, to think about this in the same terms he was.

"Look, Clint," Townsend said, "you do what you

think is best and I'll go along with it, as long as it gets me out of here."

Clint didn't have to think about that before he said, "Agreed."

When Clint walked back into the sheriff's office, the man's eyes came open and regarded him sleepily.

"Will you be staying for the hanging, señor?" he asked.

"I don't think so."

"I would think not," the man said. "It is not easy to watch a friend die."

"No," Clint said, "I suppose it isn't. Can I ask you something, Sheriff?"

The man shifted his bulk in his chair, trying to get more comfortable, and replied, "If you must."

"Did you like the dead man, your mayor?"

"Esteban Morales was not a likable man, señor," the sheriff said. "He was rude, he beat his wife—this we know—and probably his daughter, as well. He ran many businesses in town and cheated his neighbors."

"Then why would you elect him mayor?"

"He was never elected mayor, señor, he just . . . appointed himself."

"So why, if he was such a terrible man, would you sentence to death the man who shot him in self-defense?" Clint asked.

The sheriff shrugged. "It is the law, señor."

TEN

Clint left the jail and walked over to Carmen's café—which, he assumed, was one of the businesses her husband owned in town.

"Ah, you came," she said, greeting him at the door.

The place was different than it had been yesterday. Today all the tables were taken, except for one.

"I saved you a table."

"Thank you, Carmen, but how could you be sure I'd come?"

"I hoped," she said. "Please, come sit and let me bring you breakfast."

"Whatever you bring is fine with me."

"Good," she said. "I will feed you well, but first I must finish with the rest of these people."

As Clint looked around he noticed that most of them were almost done with their meals. They were giving him curious looks, and he returned the stares blankly. There were couples together, men sitting together, and men sitting alone. He noticed that most of the men were armed, some with holsters, but most with pistols tucked into their belts.

Carmen returned with coffee for him, pouring him a cup and leaving the pot.

"It looks like most of these people take being deputized seriously."

"They know the sheriff is much too fat to do anything himself."

"If that's the case why don't they fire him and hire a new sheriff?"

"That might happen," she said, "as soon as a new mayor is appointed. You see, the sheriff was my husband's handpicked man, and he would not allow him to be fired."

"I see."

"I will be back."

She hurried to accept payment from some people, to say good-bye, and to accept what appeared to be heart-felt condolences. Carmen had been absolutely right yesterday when she said that the dead always commanded respect. It was as if people conveniently forgot all the bad things someone did after he or she died. From all Clint had heard about Esteban Morales, this town should have been celebrating his death, not mourning it—and certainly not hanging a man for it.

The crowd in the place thinned out quickly, maybe because he was there—or partly so. Maybe he was taking too much credit.

She brought him his *huevos rancheros* and some tortillas, then again went to accept payment, good-byes, and condolences.

Finally, halfway through his meal, the café was suddenly empty but for him and Carmen. She came and gratefully sat in the chair opposite him.

"Is this normal for you, to be this busy?"

"It is not usually as busy as this, but not as slow as you saw it yesterday. Both were the results of my husband's death, I'm afraid. Perhaps things will return to normal after—" She stopped short and put her hand over her lovely mouth.

"After my friend is hanged?"

"I am sorry," she said. "I did not mean to say . . ."

"That's all right, Carmen," he said. "Don't worry about it. These eggs are wonderful!"

She looked around, lowered her voice, and leaned forward—affording him an excellent view of her full breasts—and said, "If you want to break your friend out of jail I will help."

He stared at her for a few moments and then decided that she was dead serious.

"I might take you up on that," he said, then quickly added, "if I decide to break him out of jail."

"It would not be difficult to do," she said, sitting back again and bringing her voice to its normal level. "You would only need to bring your horses around to the back at night. The sheriff would not be able to stop you. He would have to get out of his chair for that."

"I see you've given this some thought."

"*Sí.* I do not think your friend should suffer because Carmalita is a *puta* and her father was a pig."

"He'd be glad to hear you say that," Clint said.

"So you have only to say the word and I will be your willing accomplice."

He hated to ask the next question, but it popped into his head.

"And would you want something in return for this cooperation?"

She didn't take offense.

"I would be getting something in return," she said. "Your friend killed my husband—*Dios mio*, I will be giving *him* something in return for that. Also, I can now ask Carmalita to leave my house. Without her father around I am bound to her no longer, thanks be to God."

Clint finished his breakfast, pushed the plates away, and poured himself another cup of coffee.

"I am serious about this, Clint."

"I know you are, Carmen," he said, "and I appreciate

the offer. I just need some time to . . . think things over.''

"You must think quickly, then," she pointed out, "for your friend does not have much time."

ELEVEN

Clint decided that he'd best break his friend out without delay. He'd do it that night. Now what he needed to figure out was if he needed Carmen to do it. He would rather not risk her position in town or, if it came to shots being fired, her life. He thought he could easily go to the livery after dark, saddle both horses, bring them around to the back of the jail without being seen, and then go inside and break Townsend out. He doubted that the fat and complacent sheriff of Dos Cervezas would even try to stop him.

So, no, the answer was there was no reason to involve Carmen. However, he would hate to leave town without saying good-bye to her and thanking her for her kindness. He would also hate to leave before getting a chance to see her naked body covered with sweat caused by their lovemaking.

And there was a lot of time to go before darkness would fall.

A lot of time.

He went back to the jail carrying a tray he had gotten from Carmen. He had not yet told her that tonight would be the night. He was going to wait and go to her house after she closed the café for the day.

As he entered the jail the sheriff's face perked up as he smelled what was on the tray.

"That is Carmen's cooking," he said. "I would know that smell anywhere."

"You're right, it is."

"She sent that over for me?"

"Would I be bringing a tray here if it was for you, Sheriff?" Clint asked. "Do I look like an errand boy?"

"Well—" The man looked crestfallen.

"This is for your prisoner. Would you open his cell so I can give it to him, please?"

This made the sheriff knit his eyebrows. In order to open the cell door he'd have to get up from his chair. On the other hand, he could let Clint take the key off the wall peg and open it himself. There was no other door to this building, and no way for the two of them to escape without coming past him.

"Leave your gun," he said, "and you can go back there and open it yourself."

Clint made a show of considering this, then left his gun on the desk, took the key, and went back to the cell.

"Now?" Pete Townsend asked when he saw Clint.

"Now you eat," Clint said.

"But you have the key!" Townsend said, as Clint fitted the key into the lock.

Clint opened the door and entered with the tray.

"Now you eat," he said, adding in a low voice, "tonight you get out."

"When?"

"Late," Clint said. "After midnight. Just sit tight until then. I'll come in and get you."

Townsend grabbed his friend's arm and said, "I don't know how to thank you."

"You'll find a way."

"You're right, I will," Townsend said. "In fact, it's the reason I asked you to meet me here."

"What is?"

Townsend smiled. "I'll tell you tonight, after you get me out. After we're away from here." He turned his attention to the tray of food. "All of a sudden I've got my appetite back. This smells great."

"Enjoy it," Clint said, adding loudly, "I'll see you later, when I come back to collect the tray."

He left the cell, locked the door, and walked back into the office. He replaced the key on the wall peg and turned to face the sheriff.

"If you like," he said, "I can watch him while you go and get something to eat."

The sheriff shook his head.

"I do not think I could trust you to watch your own friend," he said.

"Suit yourself," Clint said. "I'll be back later to collect the tray."

"I thought you said you were not an errand boy."

"I'm not," Clint said, and then added, "for *you*."

TWELVE

Clint decided to wait outside the café for Carmen to close, rather than catch her at her house later. When she came out and saw him she smiled.

"I am glad you are here," she said.

"I want to come home with you."

She looked around, as if checking to see if anyone could hear them.

"I want you to," she said. "Come."

"Carmen, I've decided to take you up on your offer of help."

"Good," she said as they walked. "What would you like me to do?"

"I need some supplies," he said. "If I go in and buy them myself word might get around. If you do it, people will just think you're shopping."

"When do you need these supplies?"

"Today."

"Oh," she said. "You will be leaving, then? Tomorrow?"

"Sooner."

"Oh," she said, again.

"You're the only person in this town I trust."

She smiled and said, "I am flattered." Then she stopped abruptly.

"What is it?" he asked.

"I will have to go and get the supplies now, before the store closes."

"I can give you some money."

"There is no need," she said. "I will put it on my account."

"I'd like to pay—"

"If I pay cash for the supplies," she said, "it will look suspicious."

"Oh . . . okay, you're right."

"Besides," she said, "Esteban owned the store, so I guess I own it now . . . or I will, soon."

"That reminds me," Clint said. "Have you seen Carmalita since yesterday?"

"No," she said. "She did not come back to the house."

He frowned.

"Are you . . . worried about her?"

"More like I'm worried about what she might do," he said. "I assume a man has never turned her down before."

"Perhaps she can benefit from the experience."

"That would be nice," he said, "but from what little I know about her I don't think that's going to be the case."

"You're afraid she might do something to . . . upset your plans?"

"I expect her to try to do something to get back at me," he said.

"If she doesn't know you're leaving so soon, maybe she won't have time to do something."

"I hope not."

"Here," she said, pressing a key into his hand. "This is the key to my house. Go there and wait for me. I will come with the supplies very soon."

"Let me tell you what I need," he said. "I plan to travel light. . . ."

He went to her house and let himself in. He was immediately aware that someone else was there. The house only had one floor, so he closed the door loudly and waited to see what would happen.

Carmalita stepped into the room from a doorway.

"Oh, it's you," she said.

She was dressed very much the way she had been when he last saw her—well, that wasn't quite true. The last time he'd seen her she'd been naked, but her skirt and blouse looked like the same ones she'd had on last time he saw her dressed.

"What are you doing here?" she asked.

"I came to see your—I came to see Carmen."

"Ah!" Carmalita said. It was as if a light went on in her head.

"Ah, what?"

"Now I see why you spurned me," she said. "You are sleeping with dear Mama."

"She's not your mother."

"Dear Stepmama, then. I see she did not wait long after my father's death. *Puta!*"

Clint wanted to say she was one to talk, but he didn't want to fight with her.

"You've got Carmen all wrong, Carmalita, but I'll leave that for you and her to discuss. She was worried when you didn't come home last night."

Carmalita laughed.

"That is a lie," she said. "She was very happy when I did not come back. She would be very happy if I never came back, and I would be very happy never to see her again."

"Why are you here, then?"

"I . . . needed something."

"Like what? Money?"

The young woman didn't answer.

"Is that your room you're coming out of, or hers?" he asked.

"It was my father's room."

Clint looked at her hands, which were empty. She could have taken some money from the room and stuffed it into a skirt pocket—if her skirt had pockets. She also could have stuffed it down her cleavage. He wasn't about to search her, though.

"Where are you going now?" he asked.

"Out," she said, "just out. I will not be in your way. You and Carmen can be like animals on the floor, if you like."

"Carmalita—"

"I must go," she said, brushing past him. When she reached the door, she turned with her hand on the doorknob.

"You are the only man who ever rejected me."

"Carma—"

"I will not forget," she said, and hurriedly left, slamming the door behind her.

THIRTEEN

When Carmen came through the door, Clint hurried to help her with her packages.

"Whoa! Didn't I say I wanted to travel light?"

"I need some things for myself, too," she said, as he helped her put the packages on the table.

The house was made up of three rooms, two bedrooms and then one large room with a stove and a table and some chairs that had seen better days. Still, given that it was the home of the mayor, and that he had owned several businesses, it was probably the best house in town.

"I got you what you need," she said. "These are yours." She pushed his items off to one side, and then started putting her own items away.

"Carmalita was here when I got here," Clint told her.

She turned quickly and looked at him.

"She's gone."

"What did she want?"

"Well . . . she was coming out of that room."

"*Caramba!*" she said, and hurried into the room. When she came out she was shaking her head.

"Did she take anything?"

"A few pesos," she said. "Now she is a *puta and* a thief."

"I'm sorry," he said. "I should have stopped her."

"It is not your fault."

She went back to what she had been doing.

He enjoyed watching her move around, putting things away.

"What will you do now?" he asked.

"Do?"

"Now that you are a widow, and Carmalita might not live here anymore."

She stopped and considered.

"Well, I do not think I will live here anymore, either," she said, finally.

"Is this the mayor's house?"

She nodded and said, "Yes, so when they appoint a new mayor I will have to move."

"Will you keep the café?"

"Oh, yes," she said. "That was mine before I married Esteban."

"What about the other businesses he owned?"

"I do not know," she said. "I will have to wait and see—but I do not want to talk about that. I want to talk about what you are going to do."

"Well, I'm going to—"

"Wait," she said. "I will make some coffee and then we can talk, yes?"

"That would be great."

Over coffee he told her that he was going to do exactly what they had discussed earlier, and that he was going to do it tonight.

"I will help—"

"No," he said, hurriedly cutting her off, "you've helped enough. I can do this myself. It won't be very hard to do. I don't think the sheriff will give me very much trouble."

"He will probably be asleep by then," she said. "How will you get in?"

"Well, I get the feeling he doesn't lock the door, but if he does I'll just knock and wake him. I'll tell him I came late to get the tray. He was very disappointed this afternoon when he smelled your food and realized it wasn't for him."

"I suppose I must take part of the blame for his corpulence," she said. "My food, I mean, my cooking has helped to make Ignacio the way he is."

"Was he friends with your husband?"

"My husband had no friends. He was a terrible man. He became mayor because nobody else wanted the job."

"Why did you marry him, then?" Clint wanted to know.

She shrugged. "He was the wealthiest man in town. Not very rich by your *Norte Americano* standards, but by Mexican standards he was a wealthy man."

"So even if you can't live here anymore, you'll have some money."

"Yes," she said.

"Why don't you leave here?"

She spread her hands, looked bemused, and asked, "And go where? This is where I was born, and this is where I will die. I would not feel comfortable anywhere else."

"A woman like you, you could go anywhere and live well," he said.

"A woman like me?"

"Strong, independent, beautiful."

"Old," she added.

"You're not old."

"When I look at Carmalita," she said, "at how beautiful and full of life she is, I feel old."

"But there's something missing in her, isn't there?" he asked. "Something that is not beautiful."

"*Sí,*" Carmen said, "that is true."

"But what she is lacking is in you," he said. "That's what makes you more beautiful than she is."

"I think it is a good thing you are leaving tonight."

"Why is that?"

"Because I think you can probably talk the stars down from the heavens when you get started."

He reached across the table and took her hand.

"I don't want to talk anymore, Carmen," he said. "I'm leaving tonight, and I'd hate to waste the rest of the time we have."

"Ah," she said, with a smile, "you have another way you would like to spend that time?"

"Oh," he said, "I have an idea or two."

FOURTEEN

She led him by the hand into her bedroom, took the time
to turn down the bedclothes before turning to face him.
He put his hand on her shoulders, enjoying the smooth-
ness and warmth of her round shoulders. Gently, he
pushed the peasant blouse down further and further until
suddenly her full breasts popped into view. They were
full and heavy, with large, brown nipples that were already distended. He cupped her breasts in his palms,
used his thumbs to manipulate her nipples until she
moaned and dropped her head back. He leaned forward
and kissed her exposed neck, then moved his kisses
downward, first to the upper slopes of her breasts, then
lower, and then, finally, to the nipples. He kissed them,
teased them with his lips, his tongue, and then his teeth.
She moaned in her throat and her hands were between
them, first feeling his hardness through his pants, then
hurriedly undoing his belt.

He stopped her, taking his hands in his and gently
pushing them away. He removed his gun belt, walked
to the bedpost, and hung it there. When he turned he
saw that she had pulled the blouse over her head and
discarded it, and was tugging down the skirt. It dropped
around her ankles and she kicked away. She stood there

gloriously naked, all opulent curves and shadows—a woman's body.

He looked at the bed and said, "I don't like using another man's bed. You and your husband—"

She touched her forefinger to his lips to silence him.

"We slept here together, but there was no love in this bed. You and I, we will have love here, even if it is only for one night. Do not take that memory away from me, I beg you."

"What about Carmalita?" he asked. "If she comes back—I told her there was nothing between us. If she catches us . . . she'll think badly of you."

Carmen laughed, took his hand, and kissed it.

"You are a sweet man," she said. "Carmalita already thinks as badly of me as she can. I am not worried about her opinion."

She moved her hands to his belt and this time he did not push them away. She undid his pants so she could slide them and his underwear down to his ankles. With his help she got his boots off, then tugged away the pants and tossed them aside. While she was on her knees in front of him she took his penis in her hands, stroked it, pressed it to her cheek, then turned her head and licked him up and down, the full length of him, before finally taking him wholly into her mouth. Her head moved back and forth for a while, with one of his hands on her. She slid her hands up the inside of his thighs, around to cup his buttocks, then back around again to fondle his heavy genitals.

She released him from her mouth, then. He had removed his shirt while she was working on him and now she kissed her way up his belly to his chest, his neck, his chin, and finally his mouth. Their mouths fused together hungrily, their tongues playing like two snakes, and finally they fell onto the bed together.

Clint pushed her onto her back and began to explore

her body. He used his palms, his fingers, his lips, his mouth, his teeth, his tongue, all of which drove her into a frenzy until she started babbling in Spanish and pulling him up to her. He raised himself over her, looked down at her, and said, "You're beautiful."

She smiled and pulled his head down to kiss him. As their lips met he moved his hips and his rigid penis entered her cleanly, with no obstruction. She was very wet, and so very hot as he moved in and out of her, slowly, ever so slowly, and then faster and faster until she wrapped her full thighs around him, held him tightly to her that way and moved her hips in unison with him until they were both approaching the moment of climax and then they went over the edge together, he groaning, she laughing and kissing his face. . . .

"Never has it been like that with a man," she said. "I am not a *puta*, though I have been with many men—but never like this."

"Carmen—"

"I have never had a man so . . . so eager for me to feel pleasure. Most men are pigs who seek their own pleasure, then roll over and go to sleep. Esteban was this way, but not you."

"I'm not sleepy."

She slid her hand down between his legs and found his penis semierect.

"Dios mio," she said, "could you possibly . . . do it again?"

"Oh," he said, "with the right woman . . ."

She closed her hand over him and stroked him until—to her delight—he was fully erect again.

She shimmied down his body with delight and once again took him into her mouth. She made a noise a child might make while eating a piece of sweet candy as she suckled him wetly, and then she crawled up and sat on him, taking him deep inside of her.

"This time," she said, "we will go slower, and last longer."

Oh, they tried . . .

FIFTEEN

Clint almost paid homage to Carmen's body in his attempt to make the few hours they spent together memorable for her.

Later, while they lay together covered by a thin sheen of sweat, listening to each other's heartbeats, he wondered what would become of her once he left the town of Two Beers. What would become of Carmalita, who, if she would listen to her stepmother, could probably grow into as fine a woman as Carmen was now?

"I have to go," he said, abruptly.

"So soon?"

He laughed.

"It's been hours, Carmen," he said. "I'll be lucky if I can walk from here to the livery stable."

She put her arms around him and held him tightly to her for a long moment before releasing him.

They got up together and dressed.

"I will get your supplies," she said.

They went into the other room, and he watched as she packed his supplies into a burlap sack. He often carried supplies this way when he was traveling light, usually tying the sack to his saddle horn. Inside was coffee, beef jerky, a tin or two of beans, a slab of bacon, and some canned peaches.

She handed him the sack and placed her head against his chest. He held her for a moment.

"I will never forget you," she said, "or this night."

"I wish only good things for you, Carmen."

"*Vaya con Dios,*" she said. "God will protect you."

They walked to the door, where he paused for a moment.

"Try to get through to Carmalita, Carmen," he said, finally. "She's a lovely young girl; she just needs some guidance—and you're the one who could do it."

"She hates me," she said, "but for you, I will try."

"Good."

They embraced again, kissed, and then he opened the door and stepped out.

He walked to the livery and found that this sleepy little town was true to its image. The doors to the livery were open. Since everyone was a deputy, they did not expect anyone to steal anything. He hoped that this town would continue to go unnoticed by strangers, but he was afraid that someday soon the wrong men would come there and pick it clean.

He went inside, saddled both his horse and Pete Townsend's, then walked them outside. It was dark, with a sliver of a moon. He paused there to give his eyes time to adjust. He was glad for the sliver, and not a full moon. There was less chance that he would accidently be seen.

He led the horses to the jail, finding a route that would not take him down the center of town. There were enough alleys for him to reach the back of the jail without being seen. He tied Townsend's horse off, and simply dropped Duke's reins to the ground. The big gelding would not budge until he came back.

Now he walked around to the front of the jail. Through the window he could see the sliver of a light.

He tried the door, hoping he would not have to knock and alert the sheriff to his presence. He was happy to have the door open easily and soundlessly.

He stepped inside and closed it behind him. He could hear the slow, even breathing of the sheriff, who was asleep in his chair behind his desk, his hands folded over his corpulent belly. There were several ways he could play this. He could wake the man up and put him in the cell when he took Townsend out. Or he could simply hit him over the head. The man would wake up the next morning with a headache, but be no worse for wear. Or, given the way the man was sleeping, he could simply get the keys from the wall and take Townsend out of the jail without even waking him.

The first plan would enable the sheriff to raise the alarm from the cell. The third might find him waking too soon and also raising the alarm. He decided that it was best to go with the second way.

He walked behind the sheriff, took out his gun, and tapped him on the head just hard enough to take him from sleep to unconsciousness. He took a moment to make sure the man would not topple from his chair, then retrieved the keys from the wall and went into the back.

"Wake up, Pete! Time to go."

"I ain't asleep," Townsend said. "I been waiting for you."

Clint unlocked the door and Pete Townsend stepped out, a free man.

"What'd you do with the sheriff?"

"Made sure he wouldn't wake up until morning."

The two men went back into the office. Clint replaced the key on the wall. Townsend started going through the desk drawers for his gun.

"Don't knock him over," Clint cautioned.

"I found it!"

Townsend strapped his gun on, looked at Clint, and said, "I'm ready."

SIXTEEN

When they got a few miles out of town, Clint said, "North, over the border?"

"No, no," Townsend said, "south."

"Deeper into Mexico?"

"Right."

"Why?"

Townsend grinned and said, "I can't tell you that now. Let's ride, put some distance between us and Two Beers, and when we camp I'll tell you."

"This is the surprise you were telling me about?"

"Yep."

"Am I going to like it?"

"A whole lot."

Somehow, as they headed south, Clint doubted it.

They rode through Mexico in the dark until Townsend's horse stumbled and almost fell.

"We've got to stop before your horse steps in a chuckhole and breaks his leg," Clint said.

"What about yours?"

"Duke never steps in chuckholes."

"Why not? Too smart?"

"That . . . and his hooves are too big. Come on, let's camp."

They decided to go ahead and build a fire. Even if a posse did come out of Two Beers, it wouldn't be until morning.

"What about *rurales*?" Clint asked.

"The *rurales* won't bother us," Townsend said, sounding sure of himself.

"How do you know that?"

"Because they're crooked," Townsend said. "All we'd have to do is buy them off."

"How do you know that?"

"Because," Townsend said, "I've become a student of Mexico."

They built a fire and Clint brought out the supply sack. They made coffee and heated up some beans and sat around the fire, enjoying the makeshift meal.

"All right," Clint said, "I guess I'm ready for this surprise."

Townsend grinned, took a piece of paper out of his shirt, opened it, and passed it to Clint. Folded it had been small, but it opened up to ten times its size. Clint took a look by the light of the fire.

It was a map.

"Jesus," he said, and made as if to toss it into the fire.

"Don't do that!"

"That's what it's worth," Clint said. "Let me guess. You bought this off of some old prospector."

"No," Townsend said, "it was an old whore."

"An old whore?"

"Well, she wasn't that old, but she was out in front of the hotel I was staying in, and she had these maps for sale."

"Yeah," Clint said, "to gullible gringos like you."

"We got to talkin'," Townsend went on, "and I said

I didn't want any map to a mine. So she had somethin' else—this.''

"And what's this?"

"It's a map to Maximilian's treasure."

"Maximilian's treasure?" Clint asked. He squinted at the map, thinking he was going to have to get a better look at it in the daylight. "What treasure did Maximilian have?"

"Well, it wasn't really a treasure so much as it was a treasury," Townsend said.

"Treasury."

Townsend nodded.

"See, when Maximilian was sent here from France he was sent with a treasury."

"Cash?"

"No. There was some gold and some other items like art objects, things like, uh, cups or—what did they call them—chalices? With jewels on them?"

"Wait a minute," Clint said. "How do you know all this?"

"I told you, I've done some research," Townsend said.

"So what did Maximilian do with this treasury?"

"He didn't use it as a treasury," Townsend said. "He hid it.''

"And you have the map to show you where he hid it?"

"Right."

"Pete, if this woman had the map, why didn't she go look for it?"

"Well, she is, but she needed help."

"You?"

"And you."

"So we're on our way to meet this old whore?"

"I told you," Townsend said, "she ain't so old, but yeah.''

"So you brought me to Mexico for a treasure hunt?"

"More like a treasury hunt."

Clint stared at his friend for a moment.

"Well," Townsend said, "do you have something better to do?"

Clint thought for a moment, then had to admit that he didn't.

SEVENTEEN

During the next few days Clint received an oral history lesson about Mexico from Townsend. He had no idea if the man actually knew what he was talking about.

The gist of it was that Mexico had never accepted Maximilian as their emperor, so he'd felt no guilt about withholding this "treasury" from the people. When he realized that he was in danger of being overthrown by the forces that were following Benito Juárez, he sent his wife back to France to get help. When she got there no one would listen to her and, always a woman on the edge, she went mad and was put away. Eventually, Juárez overthrew Maximilian and had him executed.

"Juárez served as president of Mexico until 1871, when Porfirio Díaz took over. There have been two other presidents since then, but Díaz is back in power now."

"And how's he going to feel about us finding this treasury? I would think that Juárez, and Díaz, and the others would have had their armies out looking for it."

"If they know about it."

"Pete," Clint said, "if you know about it, they know about it."

"Maybe they just think it's a legend."

"And what if it is?"

"It ain't," Townsend said confidently.

"Well," Clint said, "I guess we're going to find out. Tell me why we don't have to worry about Díaz's army?"

"Because he's drastically reduced his army."

"Why?"

"Because he knows it would be useless if some foreign power wanted to conquer him, and more than useless if the United States invaded. So his army—such as it is—was used primarily to protect the country against the Indians."

"And the *rurales*?"

"The *rurales* are used to hunt down bandits, but many of them are bandits themselves. They're Díaz's rural police, keeping the peace, but they're even more corrupt than his army was."

"And they're the ones we'd have to worry about?" Clint asked.

"Not worry about," Townsend said. "They're the ones we'd have to deal with."

"Which means we'd have to buy them off."

"Right."

"And if we find this treasury, they're just going to go away?"

"Well," Townsend said, "if we find it we're not going to let them know."

"I see. And who else is going to be looking for this treasury besides you and me and this old—sorry, this ex-whore?"

"Nobody. That's the beauty of it. Nobody's been looking for it for years."

"Maybe," Clint said, "because it doesn't exist."

"If you're gonna be a pessimist about it—"

"Okay, okay, sorry," Clint said. "You're right: I have nothing else to do, so we might as well look for it."

Townsend reined in his horse abruptly, and Clint went

a few lengths ahead before also stopping. He turned in his saddle to look at his friend.

"What is it?"

"Look, Clint," Townsend said, "you don't owe me a thing, I owe you—and I owed you even before you got me out of that jail. When I decided to go after this treasury you're the only one I thought of to share it with. You know that?"

Clint thought of a few answers to that. One was, "You mean I'm the only one dumb enough to go along with you." Another was, "You mean I was the only one you wanted watching our back." But he didn't use any of those. What he said was, "I know."

Townsend rode up alongside Clint.

"Are you with me on this till the end?"

"That depends," Clint said.

"On what?"

"On who decides when the end is."

Townsend leaned over and tapped Clint on the chest.

"Tell you what," he said. "I'll leave that to you. When you say it's over, it's over."

"Are you serious?"

"Dead serious."

"Okay then," Clint said. "With that kind of control how can I say no?"

They started riding again.

"Where are we headed?" Clint asked.

"Well, I'd like to start right from the beginning."

"Where would that be?"

"Vera Cruz."

Clint whistled.

"That's a hell of a ride from here."

Vera Cruz was where Maximilian first docked when he came to Mexico from France.

"I know it is," Townsend said. "That's why we're actually gonna start someplace a lot closer."

"And where would that be?"

"Guadalajara."

"What's there?"

"It's where Maximilian finally lost his hold on the North to Díaz."

"And why are we going there?"

"It's just a jumping-off point," he said. "It's where I got the map."

"Ah," Clint said, "so it's where we're going to meet our partner."

"Exactly."

EIGHTEEN

Actually, Matamoros fell first to Juárez, then Tampico; and finally, when Guadalajara fell, that was when the Emperor Maximilian realized he had lost the North.

And he panicked.

"We believe," Townsend said, as he and Clint rode toward Guadalajara, which was now visible in the distance days after they left Two Beers, "that this is when Maximilian decided to hide his treasury."

"And why did he want to hide it?"

"He didn't want Juárez getting his hands on it," Townsend said, "and he didn't want the Mexican people getting hold of it."

"What was he going to do with it when he was out of power?"

"He was going to take it back to France with him," Townsend said. "He'd have to have money when he got there."

"But he never did."

"No," Townsend said, "he was executed first."

"Where did this happen?"

"In a town called Querétaro. Did you know that the United States pleaded for mercy on the part of Maximilian?"

"No, I didn't know that."

"Juárez thought that executing him anyway would send a message to the U.S."

"What message?"

Townsend shrugged.

"I suppose that they couldn't tell him what to do."

"Well," Clint said, "then I guess he showed us, huh?"

When they got to Guadalajara, there was not much going on.

"Siesta time," Townsend said. "Everyone will wake up refreshed and ready for the rest of the day. It's a practice I think the United States should start."

"I believe it is everyone's right," Clint said, "to choose the time of his own nap."

"Spoken like a true American," Townsend said.

They rode to a livery stable where they gave their horses over to a young man who admired Duke very much.

"Take good care of him, then," Clint warned.

"I will, señor," the boy said, "I promise."

Clint and Townsend left the livery with their saddlebags and their rifles. Townsend said they were going to a hotel called the Palace.

"How original."

On the way Townsend asked, "So do you think I'm a fugitive now?"

"If you are, so am I."

"Why? They can't prove you're the one who broke me out. The sheriff never saw who hit him."

"You're gone, I'm gone," Clint said. "They'll pretty much put the pieces together, I think."

"Yeah, but they can't *prove* it."

"Well," Clint said, "we'll have to see . . ."

•   •   •

They registered in the hotel, which was a huge three-story adobe structure that dominated the street it was on. The lobby was very large and ornate, and off to one side was a bar and a restaurant. The floor looked as if the tile had been laid by hand, one by one.

"Very impressive," Clint said. "Is this the hotel where you bought the map?"

Townsend nodded and said, "Right outside."

They went up to their rooms, which were right across from each other.

"We should probably put the rest of siesta time to good use," Townsend said. "We won't be able to get anything to eat until it's over, anyway."

They'd had to rouse the desk clerk from his slumber, and he'd been very cranky about it. As they left the desk to go to their rooms Clint heard him muttering about "crazy gringos."

"All right," Clint said, "a nap sounds good to me."

"You'll like the bed," Townsend said. "The mattresses are nice and thick."

Clint was looking forward to it. He hadn't slept on a plush mattress in quite a while.

"I'll knock on your door when I wake up and we'll get something to eat," Townsend said.

"When do I meet our partner?"

"We'll just have to wait for her to find us."

"How will she know we're here?"

"I don't know," Townsend said, just before he closed his door, "but she will."

Clint closed his own door, dropped his gear, and sat on the bed. As promised, the mattress was very thick. He lay on his back without removing his clothing or his gun belt, and fell asleep.

NINETEEN

Clint woke before Townsend knocked on his door. When he walked to the window and looked down on the square in front of the hotel, it was like a different world. It was teeming with people; if he didn't know better he would have thought he was in a different town. Clint had been to Mexico before, but he had never gotten used to siesta, the concept that an entire town could "take a nap."

He was still standing at the window when there was a knock on the door. It was Townsend.

"Ready to get something to eat?"

His friend looked well rested and clean. He had probably put the pitcher and basin in his room to good use, as Clint had done upon waking.

Out in the hall Townsend took a deep breath and said, "This is sure better than that cell I was in back in Dos Cervezas. I guess I'm never gonna be able to say thanks enough, Clint."

"You would have done the same for me," Clint said, which Townsend responded to with silence.

They stopped in the hotel dining room, which was as busy as it had been empty just hours before. A waiter met them at the door and took them to a table. They ordered enough food for four men and proceeded to put it all away in short order.

"What do we do now, Pete?" Clint asked.

"We've got to wait for Rosa to come and get us, Clint," Townsend said. "We can't do much without her."

"Why not? You've got the map, don't you?"

"You don't understand," Townsend said. "When she tells you the story of Maximilian's treasury you'll believe it. Then you'll be as sure as I am."

"I don't have to be sure to go with you, Pete," Clint said. "If we're waiting for her just so she can convince me, it's a waste of time."

"We can't go without her," Townsend repeated. "That's all there is to it."

"Okay," Clint said, "if you feel that strongly about it, we'll wait."

"Let's walk around a bit."

"I don't know how wise that is," Clint said. "Remember, you *might* be a wanted man."

"Ah," Townsend said, "I doubt that the word would have spread this far this fast. Besides, we could stop in a barbershop and I could get a haircut. And I'll grow a mustache, okay?"

Townsend touched his upper lip, where he already had several days' head start on one.

"Nobody would recognize me."

"Maybe," Clint said, "we could even take a bath."

"And then find a couple of nice, pretty, sweet-smelling señoritas, huh?"

"Let's take it one step at a time," Clint said. "A haircut and then a bath, for me."

"Fine, let's go."

"Wait, maybe the hotel has a service—"

"We want to see the town, don't we?"

"You've been here before, remember?" Clint asked.

"Well, I, uh, didn't get to see very much of it last time."

"Why not?"

"I was kind of busy."

"Doing what?" Clint asked suspiciously.

"Staying out of trouble."

"That's a full-time job for you."

"Well," Townsend said, "now I've got you to help me with it, don't I?"

"I don't think that's what I signed on for," Clint said, "but like I said before, let's just take it one step at a time."

"Okay," Townsend said. "Step one is to get out of this hotel. Come on."

Out on the street they found it impossible to get into the flow of the foot traffic. For one thing, they stood out as gringos; for another, the rhythm that the Mexican people kept was alien to them.

"I can't even walk like them," Clint said. "We might need some new clothes, Pete, if we're going to blend in."

"Like sombreros?" Townsend asked, frowning. "I hate those things. Don't know how anyone can wear them."

"They keep the sun out of your face."

"I like the sun on my face."

"Well," Clint said, "maybe we don't need sombreros. Maybe a couple of serapes will do the trick. We'll see if we can buy some after we take a bath."

They found a barbershop several blocks from the hotel and away from the square. It was less busy here and the barber was able to take them right away, first Townsend, then Clint. After that he had a couple of small boys fill bathtubs up with hot water for them in the back, and they were able to soak virtually side by side. They each pulled a chair over to their tubs and hung their gun belts on the back, within easy reach.

"Nothing like hot water . . ." Clint started to say, but when he looked over at Townsend he saw that his friend had fallen asleep. He decided to leave him that way unless he was in danger of drowning.

Somehow, he didn't think he was getting the whole story from Townsend. All of this stuff about Maximilian having a hidden treasury was all well and good, but Clint couldn't believe that they were the only ones looking for it. There was more to this story than met the eye, and he was going to have to keep working on Townsend until he could squeeze it out of him.

Suddenly, as Clint reached for the soap, the door to the room opened and two men brandishing shotguns ran in. The only thing that saved Clint and Townsend was that the men had to stop and look to make sure they knew where their targets were.

"Pete!" Clint shouted, and grabbed for his gun. He cursed because his hand was slippery with soap, but he managed to get the gun out of the holster and fire at one of the men just as he fired with his shotgun.

Clint's shot took the man in the gut, driving him back and then down. The buckshot that was in the shotgun was unable to penetrate the porcelain bathtub that Clint was in.

Townsend came awake immediately, grabbed his gun, and shot the second man just as he pulled the trigger on his shotgun. The buckshot took a huge chunk out of the ceiling. By the time the debris fell on the man he was lying on his back, dead.

"The door!" Clint said.

"I got it."

They both leaped out of their tubs, and Townsend ran to the door, naked and wet, to see if there were any more assailants. He turned and looked at Clint, who was also naked and wet. Both of them were still holding their guns.

"Well," Townsend said, "if there wasn't two dead men on the floor this might actually be funny."

TWENTY

"Now what?" Townsend asked.

"Well," Clint said, "first we get dressed so that the first wave of people who come looking to see what happened don't catch us naked."

Townsend sneaked another look out the door.

"I don't see a wave," he said. "I don't even see one person."

"That can't be," Clint said. "Somebody must have heard something." He was hastily getting dressed, hopping around on one leg.

Townsend grabbed his pants and pulled them on, then checked the door again.

"Nobody's coming."

"Maybe the barber called for the law," Clint said. "Would that be a sheriff, or the *rurales*?"

"Could be either one," Townsend said, "but right now it's no one."

They finished dressing and still no one had appeared.

"All right, then," Clint said. "Let's see if we can figure out who these guys are—or were."

They rolled the two bodies over and looked at them.

"I don't know them," Clint said. "Do you?"

"No."

"Think hard, Pete," Clint said. "You didn't see these two the last time you were here?"

"I swear I don't remember seeing any of them."

"Anyone ever try to kill you before in this town?"

"No."

Clint knelt to go through their pockets, but didn't even find a peso.

"Either they weren't paid up front," he said, standing, "or they were and left the money somewhere else."

"Paid by who, though?" Townsend asked.

"That's the question."

"Maybe they weren't paid. Maybe even down here somebody recognized you."

"It's possible," Clint said, "but I'm sure that one of them was after me, and the other one was after you."

"I think you're right."

Clint reloaded his gun, ejecting the empty shell and replacing it with a live one. Townsend did the same.

"Still no law," Clint said, "and where's that damned barber?"

"You thinkin' what I'm thinkin'?" Townsend asked.

"That he set us up?"

Townsend nodded.

"Let's ask him."

They went out the door and down the hall to the front of the building. There was no one there—no customers, no barber.

"Take a look outside," Townsend said.

Clint went to the door.

"You see a dozen *rurales* waitin' for us across the street?"

"No."

"A sheriff and some deputies?"

"No."

"What *do* you see?"

"People walking by, calm as you please." Clint turned away from the door and looked at his friend.

"You don't suppose people around here actually mind their own business?"

"Now there's a thought."

Clint looked out the door again, this time higher, at balconies and at rooftops. He didn't see anybody. He turned and walked back to Townsend. They each sat down in a barber's chair.

"What do we do now?" Townsend asked. "Just walk away and leave them?"

"Unless we want to bring it to someone's attention that we killed two men," Clint said. "Two Mexican men."

Townsend shook his head. "Not me."

"Then we leave."

"By the front door?"

"I don't see any reason not to."

"Me, neither."

They waited a beat and then they both said, "Back door."

TWENTY-ONE

They found their way to the rear of the building, located the back door, and opened it slowly. Just because there was no one waiting to blow their heads off in the front didn't mean there wasn't somebody in back—but there wasn't.

"Let's go," Clint said, leading the way out.

They moved along the backs of some buildings until they came to an alley, which they cut through and took to the street.

"Where to now?" Townsend asked.

"Let's keep moving for now," Clint replied. "We need a place to talk."

"The hotel?"

"Too far," Clint said. "We need someplace where we can talk now."

They came out onto a busier street, which made Clint nervous. If two men had been sent to kill them, there could be more, and a crowded street like this could hide a multitude of killers with knives or guns—especially if the assassins were Mexicans.

"There's a cantina," Townsend said, pointing across the street. "I could use a drink after putting a bullet in a man I don't know, how about you?"

"That's as good a place as any."

This time Townsend led the way. The cantina was about half full, and didn't seem to offer anything at all in the way of entertainment, which explained that.

They went to the bar and the bartender gave them a baleful stare from behind a huge, well-oiled handlebar mustache.

"Dos cervezas," Townsend said.

The bartender nodded and supplied them with two beers. Clint surveyed the room and saw an empty table in a corner. He headed for it, Townsend in tow, and sat so he had an unobstructed view of the entire room.

"What's going on, Pete?" he asked.

"Whataya mean?"

"I mean why did somebody try to kill us the first day we got here?"

"I don't know."

"I think you do."

"You think I'm lyin' to you?"

"I think you're holding something back," Clint said. "Is that so unusual, given our past history?"

Townsend lowered his head and said, "No." Then he looked at Clint, grinned, and added, "You got too damn long a memory."

"Tell me a story, Pete."

"I told you a story, Clint. It's all true."

"Maximilian's treasury?"

"True."

"You got the map from a whore?"

"True."

Clint leaned forward.

"Nobody else is looking for it?"

Townsend sat back.

"Well . . . that might not be true. I mean, there *might* could be somebody looking for it, but I don't know for sure—I mean, ya know, I don't know names."

"What do you know?"

"Probably not as much as Rosa does."

"And how well do you know Rosa?"

"Well, after she showed me the map we sort of got friendly."

"Friendly enough that she might send someone to kill you?"

"No," Townsend said, "not Rosa. She wouldn't try to have me killed. We're partners."

"What if while you've been gone she got herself a new partner?"

Townsend opened his mouth to protest, then closed it, then opened it again, then closed it again, looking thoroughly confused.

"N-naw," he finally said. "Uh-uh, not Rosa."

"Because you know her so well?" Clint asked. "What if you're not the only gringo with a map, Pete?"

"You'll see," Townsend said. "When Rosa shows up and you talk to her, you'll see. You'll believe her, too. You'll believe in the treasury."

Clint wondered if Townsend believed in it because he wanted to, or because there was some sweet talk involved.

They worked on their beers, bought a second one each, and then Townsend suggested they go back to the hotel. The cantina was less than half full now. It was getting to be that time when men wanted to go someplace that did have entertainment—girls, gambling, or both.

"Rosa can't find us if we're here," Townsend said.

"It must be safe to leave now," Clint said. "Even if there were some other men looking for us, they've probably given up by now."

As they stood to leave, Townsend said, "You'll see, Clint. When you meet her, you'll see."

"I'll go into it with an open mind, Pete," Clint said, and then added, "and wide-open eyes, too."

TWENTY-TWO

When they got back to the hotel, the clerk at the front desk called to Townsend, "Señor? A message for you."

"Thanks."

Townsend accepted the slip of paper, and then he and Clint went off to a corner of the ornate lobby to read it.

"Who's it from?" Clint asked.

"Rosa," Townsend said. "She wants us to meet her tonight, at midnight, at the northwest corner of the square."

"Tonight?"

Townsend nodded and put the note away in his pocket.

"Why there? Why not here?"

"I don't know," Townsend said.

"What if it's a trap?"

"You're still thinking that Rosa might have sent those men to kill us?"

"I'm still entertaining the possibility, yes," Clint said.

"Look, we're meeting in the square, Clint," Townsend said. "What can happen there?"

"The square is deserted at siesta time," Clint pointed out. "What's it going to be like at midnight?"

87

"A lot busier than it is at siesta time, believe me," Townsend said.

"I don't like it."

"Relax," Townsend said.

"Look," Clint said, in what he thought was a reasonable tone of voice, "if she's not setting us up for a trap, then she's not meeting us here because somebody is looking for her."

"Okay, then," Townsend said. "I like that possibility better. Maybe it's the same somebody who sent those men to kill us. If that's the case, then she's gonna need our help, our protection."

"You know," Clint said, "when this story got started she was an old whore selling maps in front of the hotel. Now what is she, some kind of freedom fighter looking to fund a revolution with Maximilian's own treasury?"

Townsend looked away.

"Jesus Christ," Clint said, awestruck. "That's it, isn't it? I hit it."

"You're crazy."

"No, I'm not," Clint said. "I can tell by the look on your face. She recruited you to help her find the treasury because she and her people need it as a war chest—and you recruited me!"

"You think I'm that noble?" Townsend asked. "That I'd go after a treasury and not want any of it for myself?"

Clint thought a moment, then said, "No, you're right, you wouldn't do that."

Townsend nodded his agreement.

"So you're in it for the girl, and for a piece of the action."

Townsend chewed his lip for a few moments, and remained silent.

"Jesus, Pete, you're using me."

"Would you have agreed to help if I told you I

wanted you to come to Mexico to help fight a revolution?''

"I don't know," Clint said. "You never gave me the chance to find out, did you? You started lying to me from the beginning."

"Not lying . . . exactly."

"What would you call it?"

"I was just . . . stringing you along until we got here and I could tell you the truth."

"And when were you going to do that?"

"As soon as I introduced you to Rosa."

"Well," Clint said, "now you'll have your chance, if somebody doesn't kill her, or us, first."

"Clint," Townsend said, "I know that can't happen with you around. Look how quick you reacted in that barbershop. I know I can count on you to keep us alive until we find that treasury."

Clint didn't say anything.

"You *are* still gonna help us find it, aren't you?" Townsend asked.

"I don't know," Clint replied. "I'll decide after I meet your map lady."

"I can cut you in for a piece," Townsend said. "I never intended for you to do this for nothing."

"I came down here because you're my friend, Pete," Clint said. "I was willing to help you for nothing."

"Yeah, but you didn't know then that there was a fortune involved."

"Speaking of which," Clint said, "have you ever dealt with rebels before? Revolutionaries?"

"No, why?"

"Because they're very single-minded, Pete," Clint said. "All they think about is their revolution. And they're usually not too eager to share the spoils."

"Hey," Townsend said, "I made my deal with Rosa, and she'll stick to it."

"Maybe she will," Clint said, "but how about the people she works for? Will they stick to it?"

TWENTY-THREE

Since there had already been one attempt on their lives—although Townsend still clung to the belief that someone must have recognized "The Gunsmith," even here in Mexico—they decided to spend the rest of the day and evening in their rooms until their meeting with Rosa.

Clint spent most of his time wondering how the hell he had gotten tangled up with Mexican revolutionaries—but a better question was, how had Pete Townsend gotten himself involved? Townsend had been right asking Clint if he thought his friend was "that noble." Noble was certainly not a word Clint would have applied to Pete Townsend. If, indeed, it was the woman who had gotten him involved more than the money, that had not stopped him from getting into trouble with Carmalita in the town of Two Beers. How, Clint wondered, would Rosa react if she knew that? Would she care at all? Or was she just playing Townsend along to get his help—and if that was the case, why Pete Townsend?

Clint decided that all the questions that were rattling around inside his head would have to wait for their midnight meeting to be answered.

• • •

91

At a quarter to midnight there was a knock on his door. Clint opened it and stepped into the hallway to join Pete Townsend.

"Ready?" Townsend asked.

"I've been ready."

As they walked down the hall and descended the stairs to the main floor, Townsend said, "Now, one thing, Clint. Don't be impatient with Rosa."

"Is she someone I could easily become impatient with?" Clint asked.

"Well," Townsend said, "considering you're my friend, and you hardly ever lose patience with me, maybe not; but as a rule she's not in the habit of getting right to the point, you know?"

"I don't know," Clint said, "but I guess I'm going to find out."

They moved past the dozing desk clerk, went out the door, and stepped into the square.

Clint saw immediately that Townsend was right about the square. There was more activity there at midnight than there had been at midday, during siesta time. There were certainly more people walking around, even if the businesses around them were closed.

People they passed in the street did not seem to pay any attention to them. Clint kept alert, but spotted no one lurking in the shadows. He knew that if someone wanted them dead enough to shoot from a rooftop, they'd probably be dead by now.

"This must be the corner," Townsend said.

Clint was surprised. They found themselves standing in front of a small church—a chapel, really—that actually was not on the square. The side of the building faced the square, so that the front of the chapel was really around the corner.

"Where is she, then?" Clint asked.

"We still have a few minutes."

More than a few minutes passed and still Rosa did not appear.

"I'm getting a bad feeling," Clint said. "Are you sure the note was from her?"

"I don't know," Townsend said. "I've never seen her handwriting before."

"Maybe you have."

"Where?"

"On the map."

"You think she drew the map?"

"If it's a fake. Do you have it on you?"

"Yeah, but it's too dark to compare here. No, no, the message was from her."

"Then I have a suggestion."

"What is it?"

"I doubt that she'd want to meet right here out in the open."

"Then why pick this corner?"

"Maybe she thought we'd be smart enough to check inside the church."

Townsend looked at the church and said, "Well, let's do it, then, since one of us *was*."

They walked around to the front of the church and ascended the steps to the front doors. They were large and thick, made of oak. Clint grasped the handle of one and pulled it open. It seemed to be pretty dark inside, and the two friends exchanged a look.

"Do you think someone would set a trap inside a church?" Townsend asked.

"I don't know, Pete, but I guess we're about to find out."

TWENTY-FOUR

Once they were inside the church they realized it was not dark, it was simply lit by candles up near the altar, which they had not been able to see from the front. Still, at Clint's insistence, they waited just inside the door for their eyes to get used to the dimness.

"All right," Clint said, when he felt he could see well enough, "let's go."

"It looks like there's someone in the front pew," Townsend said.

"Go ahead," Clint said. "I'll be right behind you."

Townsend led the way and Clint followed, looking around carefully. To some people it wouldn't matter at all that this was a church.

As they got closer to the front they could see that the figure seated there was wearing something to cover its head.

It was probably a woman, but Clint prepared himself for anything.

"I was wondering when you would come inside," the woman said.

When she looked up at Townsend the man smiled, and it was a smile Clint had never seen on his face before. At that moment Clint knew that his friend was in love.

He also believed that the same was not true of the woman.

"Clint Adams," Townsend said, "this is Rosa Flores."

Rosa turned her head a bit further to look at Clint. Her eyes were steady on him as she appraised him.

"How much does he know?" she asked.

"I know that I've been lied to," Clint said, "and I know that I don't like it."

Rosa smiled. "You will take some convincing, then."

"Probably."

She stood up. She was tall for a woman, almost as tall as Townsend, but still several inches shorter than Clint.

"Come with me, both of you."

The stepped out of the pew and then ascended to the altar. She did not stop there, though. She led them around the altar, touched something, and a slab of the stone wall swung open.

"This way," she said, and stepped into the secret passage.

Townsend followed her without hesitation. Clint took one last look around the church, and then followed his friend.

"Where does this lead?" he asked.

"Down," she said. "There are many such passages beneath this city."

"Who knows about them?"

"Everyone."

Then, why were they being used by revolutionaries? Clint thought.

She led them along the passage, which was also lit by candles, and down a stairway. At the bottom, she knocked on a door, which was opened by a tall, painfully thin Mexican.

"You brought them here?"

"Never mind, Manuel," she said. "This is the gringo we have been waiting for, the famous Gunsmith."

Manuel looked Clint up and down, then stepped back to let them enter.

Inside Clint smelled coffee. He was about to ask for some when Rosa removed her shawl from her head and shook out her black hair. Clint had to admit that Mexican women were among the most beautiful. Anyone who needed proof only had to look at Carmalita, Carmen, and now Rosa.

Rosa was between Carmalita's and Carmen's ages, which put her at about thirty. She certainly did not look like an old whore.

"Why are you staring?" she asked him.

"Uh, you don't fit the description Pete gave me."

"Ah," she said, "I was dressed as an old whore, then. No one is pitied, or ignored, more than an old whore. I hear much when I am dressed that way."

"I smell coffee," Clint said. "If this is going to take long, I think I would like some."

"Manuel," Rosa said.

The room was not large, and the four of them were the only ones in it. It was damp, but well lit by torches rather than candles.

"Is there another way out of this room besides the door we came in?" Clint asked.

"Yes," Manuel said, handing him a cup of coffee, "but it is a secret."

"As long as it's there," Clint said. "I just hate the idea of being trapped in here."

"These passages are thought to be long deserted," Rosa said. "The *rurales* have not yet come down here looking for us."

"Rosa," Clint said, "you told Manuel that I was the man you have been waiting for. Tell me, what did Pete promise you?"

"Rosa—"

"Let her answer, Pete."

Rosa looked at them both curiously, then said, "He promised that his longtime amigo, the Gunsmith, would come and help us overthrow the dictator Díaz and take back our country for the people of Mexico."

"That's all he promised you, huh?"

"Sí," she said, "that, and that you would help us find the treasury of Maximilian."

TWENTY-FIVE

"Before Clint can do that," Townsend said, "he has to be convinced that there *is* a treasury. Also, certain . . . arrangements will have to be made—"

"Another greedy gringo!" the man spat.

"Quiet, Manuel," Rosa said. "Neither of these men are from our country. We cannot expect them to risk their lives for it without some . . . compensation."

"I've already made my deal," Townsend said.

"And you, Señor Adams?" Rosa asked. "What is your deal?"

"I think I'd like to talk about my deal with you, Rosa, away from these two."

"All right," she said, grabbing her shawl. "We can go someplace else."

"What am I supposed to do?" Townsend asked.

"Wait at the hotel," Clint said.

"Where are you two going?"

"Someplace to talk," Rosa said, putting her shawl back on. "Why don't you stay here and talk to Manuel?"

Rosa led Clint out the door as Townsend and Manuel eyed each other warily. He followed her back up the stairs and into the church.

"Aren't you afraid someone will see us coming out from behind the altar?"

"The church doors were locked after you came in," Rosa said. "No one can wander in. Come, there's a side door we can use."

When they got outside, she said, "Where shall we go to talk?"

"Someplace safe for you, I guess."

"I know the place," she said. "We can walk."

"All right."

"But I don't think we should talk until we get there."

"Why not?"

"I want to be able to see your face when we do."

"You talk like I've been the one who's been lying," Clint said.

"I have not lied to you."

"You haven't had a chance," Clint said. "So far only my friend Pete has lied."

"What did he say . . . about me?"

"Well, he started out by telling me you were an old whore who sold him a map."

"Actually," Rosa said, "I was a young whore, but I haven't been for a long time. How is that for telling the truth?"

"It's a good start," he said.

Rosa took Clint to a small cantina that, though open, didn't seem to be doing much business.

"It is owned by one of our people," she said. "He serves terrible whiskey and beer so that no one will come here."

"Is that what we're going to have?"

She smiled and said, "I will tell him to serve something drinkable." She went to the bar to talk to the bartender briefly, then led Clint to a table against the wall. Once they were seated she removed the shawl from her head. The bartender came over and put two beers in front of them.

"Do not be afraid, señor," he said. "This is not what I serve the customers."

"Thank you."

Clint sipped the beer. It was cold and good. He watched as Rosa had a sip of hers, then licked her upper lip. He reminded himself that Pete Townsend was involved with this woman.

"What would you like to know, señor?"

"First, I want you to know that Pete Townsend had no right to speak for me."

"He did not."

"He didn't?"

"He said that he would talk to you and try to get you to help us," she said. "He never came out and said that you would."

"I see."

"He said that I would have to convince you to do that on my own."

"Well, I came to Mexico in the first place to help him," Clint said, "but I didn't know that helping him would mean I'd be helping revolutionaries."

"Patriots."

"Whatever you call yourselves."

"Señor, we do not wish you to fight for us," she said, "even though we know your gun would carry much weight."

"What *do* you want from me, then?" he asked.

"We only want you to help us find Maximilian's treasury."

"Now, come on, Rosa," he said. "Isn't that just a story you told Pete to get him to help you?"

"Why would I do that?" she asked. "Is he so famous a man in your country that people try to trick him into helping them?"

"Well, no," Clint said, "he's not famous at all."

"Then why would I have lied to him?"

"Maybe to get to me."

"How would I know he was a friend of yours?"

Another point in her favor.

"I don't know."

"Please, señor," she said, "if you would just listen to me for a few moments perhaps we would better understand each other."

"All right," he said, sitting back and folding his arms, "go ahead and talk."

TWENTY-SIX

She talked for a long time, and Clint could see what Townsend meant when he said she took a long time to get to the point. She told him about dictators, about Maximilian and Juárez and Díaz and how the people of Mexico had never had a leader who was for the people. And she talked about a revolution needing funding, and how the hidden treasury of Maximilian would provide that funding.

"So you see," she said, "we need to find that treasury."

"You've talked for a long time, Rosa," Clint said, "but what you've given me is a history lesson—a history I already knew. Tell me why you think there's a hidden treasury out there."

"Because," she said, "when Juárez executed Maximilian it was never found."

"Maybe it didn't exist."

"No. We know that Maximilian came from France with a treasury. That is fact."

"Maybe he spent it all."

"He could not have," she said. "He was under scrutiny the whole time."

"Then if that's the case, what happened to it?"

"He must have hidden it," she said, "because nothing was found—nothing!"

Clint had to admit that Juárez should have found something in the treasury once he executed Maximilian and moved into the palace.

"It is out there," she said, "enough to buy us all the guns and supplies we need."

"And men."

"What?"

"You need it to buy men for your revolution."

She looked away.

"We have men."

"Not enough, though," he said. "Not enough to go and look for the treasury yourself. I think you have men who are waiting for you to show them you can fund a revolution before they'll agree to take part in it."

She kept her eyes averted.

"You wish you had men who would fight just for the love of your country," he went on, "but that's not the case, is it?"

She hesitated then said, "Yes," and looked at him. "Yes, you are right. The days of the patriot are gone. Now they want to be paid to fight."

"Like Townsend."

She waved a hand.

"I needed Townsend to get to you. You were right about that, too."

"How did you know that he knew me?"

"He bragged about it," she said. "He bragged like a little boy trying to impress me."

"And you didn't think he was lying?"

She shrugged.

"I thought I would give him the opportunity to prove he wasn't . . . and he did. You are here. You are a legend of the American West, Mr. Adams. We need you to find the legendary treasury of Maximilian."

"What about the map you gave Townsend?"

"Maps," she said. "We have many maps."

"So you gave him one, just to give him something to hold onto."

"I was always giving him something to hold onto."

"He thinks he's in love with you."

She laughed.

"A man like Pete Townsend does not love one woman. I think you know that."

Clint thought about Carmalita and nodded. He did know that, and she knew it, but did Pete Townsend know it?

"But even if he does think he loves me," she said, "he still wanted to work out a deal where he would get paid for his services."

"Paid for producing me."

"Yes," she said, "paid for producing you. And now we must work out your deal. How much do you want, Señor Adams, to help us? What is your price?"

He took his time forming his answer. He knew what he was going to tell her about his price, but he still wasn't sure what he was going to do or say beyond that.

"I don't have a price, Rosa."

She laughed, a totally humorless sound.

"All men have their price, señor," she said. "Mexican men, American men, you all want something. Gold? Me, perhaps? Would you like me to go to your hotel room with you?"

"I thought your whoring days were over, Rosa."

Anger turned her face red.

"It is not whoring if I am doing it for my country," she said.

"What's it called, then?"

"Sacrifice."

"Well," he said, "you sure don't have to make that sacrifice with me, Rosa."

"Then what?" she asked. "What do you want?"

"How can I say what I want when I haven't even said I will help?"

"Will you?"

"I don't know yet, Rosa," Clint said. "I guess I'm going to have to give it some thought."

TWENTY-SEVEN

When they left the cantina Clint asked, "Can I walk you anywhere?"

She looked at him for a long moment, then said, "No, thank you. I will contact you at your hotel tomorrow night. You can give me your decision then."

"What if I'm not ready to decide by then?" he asked.

She shrugged.

"We will have to go on without you, then," she said. "We have waited too long now."

"Wait, Rosa."

"Yes?"

"If the map you gave to Pete is no good, do you even know where to look for the treasury?"

"That is a question I will answer," she said, "when you have decided to help us."

"That's fair," he said.

"Good night, señor."

"Good night."

He watched her walk away until she had melted into the darkness, then turned and walked to his own hotel.

As soon as he entered the Palace he saw Pete Townsend sitting on one of the lobby sofas. When Townsend saw

Clint, he bounded up and came running to him, then looked past him.

"Where's Rosa?"

"She's not with me."

"She *was* with you."

"Yes, but not anymore."

"What happened?"

"Not much. We talked."

"That's all you did?"

Clint wondered if Townsend was looking at him suspiciously.

"What else would we do, Pete?"

"Nothing," he said quickly, looking away. "I didn't mean nothing." He looked at Clint again. "Did she convince you of anything?"

"Not really," Clint said. "I'm convinced that she thinks there is a treasury, but I'm not convinced there is one."

"Did you tell her you'd help her?"

"No."

"Why not?"

"Because I don't like being tricked, Pete," Clint said. "I don't like being lied to, especially not by friends. An old friend recently died, and he just about had a lie on his lips right to the end."

"I only did that for her, Clint," Townsend said. "You saw her. She's beautiful."

"Not so beautiful that you'd work for her for nothing, though."

"Well . . ."

"Not so beautiful that you were able to keep your hands off of Carmalita in Two Beers."

"Okay," Townsend admitted, "so I'm weak when it comes to beautiful women. You like them, too."

"Yes, I do," Clint said, "and I've even made a fool of myself over a woman once or twice—but not in a very long time."

"Is that what you think I'm doin'?" Townsend asked. "Makin' a fool of myself over her?"

"I think it's a possibility, yes."

"Well," Townsend said, sticking out his jaw, "I'm gonna help her, no matter what you think."

"That's fine," Clint said, "you do that."

"What are you gonna do?"

"I told her I'd think it over and give her my decision by tomorrow night."

"Is she going to come here?"

"I don't know. She said she'd contact us here. I don't know exactly what that meant."

Townsend rubbed his jaw.

"Pete, I'm going to get some sleep. It's been a long day."

"I think I'll sit down here for a while," Townsend said. "She might show up here."

"Suit yourself. Just keep alert."

"I will."

Clint started for the steps, but Townsend grabbed his arm.

"Clint?"

"Yeah?"

"I'm sorry for the lies," Townsend said. "I really am."

Clint looked at his friend and then smiled.

"Pete, it's okay, as long as your lies don't get me killed," he said. "The moment they do, I'll never forgive you."

"That sounds fair."

"And with my dying breath," Clint added, "I'll tell Rosa all about Carmalita."

"Hey," Townsend said to Clint's retreating back, "now that's not fair!"

TWENTY-EIGHT

Clint went to his room, turned down his bed, removed everything but his underwear, and crawled between the sheets. This hotel had the best mattress he'd slept on in a long time. He was just settling into it when there was a knock at his door. He toyed with the idea of ignoring it, but it had to be Townsend—who else could it be? No one else knew that he was there.

He got out of bed, walked to the door without bothering to pull on his pants, and opened it.

"This better be good—" he started, then stopped when he saw Rosa there.

"I hope it is," she said.

"Rosa . . ."

"May I come in?"

"I'm not dressed."

"It does not bother me if it does not bother you," she said.

"Well . . ." he said, then backed away from the door. "Come in. Let me get my pants on—"

"Please, not because of me," she said. "I have seen men in many stages of dress and undress, and I do not mean when I was whoring."

"Fighting?" he asked.

She nodded.

"When you fight side-by-side with men, they are not shy," she said, "especially when you are tending to their wounds."

"I guess not," he said. "Well, I'm not wounded, so I'll just put them on—"

"If I get my way, Clint," she said, slowly, "you will just have to take them off again."

He stopped with his pants in his hand, turned his head to look at her.

"Rosa, do you mean . . . ?"

"Yes," she said, "I do. Does it surprise you that I would want to share your bed?"

"Well," he said, "I thought you and Pete—"

"No," she said, "He wishes it, but I do not."

"He's down in the lobby, waiting for you."

"I saw him there," she said. "I came in the back."

"Rosa, he's my friend."

"I am not his woman."

"But—"

"Even if I was," she continued, "he could not be trusted around other women."

"You know that about him?"

"But of course . . . I know men," she said. "I know what kind of man he is."

"He's a good man."

"Yes, but weak when it comes to beautiful women."

"Aren't all men?"

"Are you?"

"Well . . ."

"Do you think I am beautiful?"

She'd taken the shawl from her head when she entered and now she placed her hands on her hips and sucked in her stomach. The dress she wore was plain and probably a size or two too big, but it could not hide the proud thrust of her breasts or the graceful swell of her hips.

"You know you are."

"Then perhaps you will be weak with me."

"Rosa," he said, "this isn't—"

"This has nothing to do with our earlier conversation, Clint," she said. "I am not here as a revolutionary; I am here as a woman."

"Rosa, still, this probably isn't a good idea."

"Why not?" she asked. "Don't you want me? Don't you find me . . . desirable?"

"Any man would be a fool not to desire you."

"I told you I know men, Clint," she said, "and you are no fool."

He didn't have an answer for that.

"Why do you hesitate?" she asked. "Perhaps I am too forward? You like more timid women? Women who will wait for you to make the first move?"

"That's not it at all."

"I do not have the luxury of waiting," she went on. "Tomorrow I could be dead, *verdad*? Or you?"

"Yes," he said, "or me."

"We face that every day, you and I," she said. "For different reasons, perhaps, but we share that."

"Yes, we do."

"Then why shouldn't we share something else?" she asked, unbuttoning her dress. "Why not share something beautiful?"

He watched as she shrugged the dress off, then shed her underclothes until she stood naked in the center of the room, illuminated by the moonlight coming in the window. He hadn't turned up the lamp on the wall when he walked to the door because the light of the moon had been enough. Now that light turned her body to silver, created shadows, . . .

"Come," she said, holding out her arms, "one night is all I ask. . . ."

Who was he to refuse?

TWENTY-NINE

Clint pushed away any guilt he may have felt about Pete Townsend as he reached for Rosa. She was right. She wasn't Townsend's woman, and Townsend had lied to Clint to get him here to meet Rosa. What did the man think would happen?

Clint took Rosa into his arms and her skin burned him. Her nipples were as hard as pebbles; her breasts—firm and round—crushed against his chest as he kissed her. Her mouth was as hot or hotter than her skin, her tongue alive in his mouth. He slid his hands down the line of her back until he reached her buttocks, full and firm, and he cupped them and pulled her against him. His erection, still inside his underwear, was crushed between them.

"Let me . . ." she said, and went to her knees in front of him. She tugged down his underwear and his erection sprang free. She gasped, then laughed and took it in her hand, stroking it, licking the underside, then taking him into her mouth. Her days as a whore were obviously not wasted as she expertly sucked him. Before she could finish him, though, he pulled her to her feet and pushed her onto the bed. Kneeling on the mattress, he drove his rigid penis into her. She was wet, and he slid into her cleanly. He grabbed her by the ankles and spread her legs even wider. He drove himself into her that way, harder and harder until the bed bounced with the impact. She gasped, reached for him but *couldn't* reach him. He was kneeling straight up between the legs he still held widespread. She wanted to hold him but couldn't, and finally just took a handful of sheet in each hand and cried out each time he drove into her, over and over and over. . . .

"I have never been . . . spread . . . that way before," she said. "It was as if you were in me as far as . . . as here." She touched herself between her breasts. "You filled me completely."

"Did I hurt you?"

"No, no," she said, "you did not. You gave me just what I wanted, just what I came for. I wanted you to . . . to fill me . . . to *ful*fill me, and you did."

They were lying in the bed together, her head on his shoulder, his left arm around her. She had tried to lie on his right arm, but he wouldn't let her, and she understood why.

"How did you get involved in this, Rosa?" he asked.

"In what?"

"Being a revolutionary."

"My parents fought Maximilian for Juárez," she said. "Then when Juárez took power they fought against him. I fought for Díaz, and when Díaz took power and betrayed us, I took up the fight against him."

"Why is it, that after revolutionaries get their man in, they decide to fight him, as well?"

"If they would keep their promises we would not fight them," she pointed out. "They promise us everything so that we will fight alongside them, and then they forget the promises once they're in power."

"We have that in my country, too," he said, "only without the fighting. We call it politics."

"And your people stand for this?"

"We live in a democracy," Clint said. "If we don't like the way a man serves while he's in office, we don't vote for him next time. We only have one problem."

"What is that?"

"One politician is as bad as another."

"Then why don't men like you run for office?"

"Well, first, nobody would vote for me," he said. "And second, I'm too smart to ever want to be a politician."

"So the men who become your politicians are the ones who are not smart enough?"

"Exactly."

She thought a moment, and then said, "I think I would rather fight than vote. Your way does not make much sense to me."

"Less people die," he said. "That's the only thing about it that does make sense."

THIRTY

Rosa stayed the night and they made love several more times before the sun came up. When it did she sat up and put her feet on the floor.

"Leaving?"

"I must," she said, "before it gets any later."

"The sun just came up."

"I know," she said. "I do not want to be seen."

"Why?" he asked, as she reached for her clothes. She bent over and her full breasts swayed before him as she pulled her dress back on. "Are you afraid your reputation will be ruined?"

"What reputation?"

"Oh, I don't know," he said. "Maybe as the madonna of the revolution? Are you not supposed to be a woman, with a woman's needs and desires?"

"You speak as if I am some great leader of the revolution," she said. "I am simply one person."

"Then who do you report to?" he asked. "Who are you trying to put in power now, Rosa?"

"That is not important now."

"Then what is?"

Fully dressed, she turned to face him. The beautiful, sensual, loving woman who had been in bed with him all night was gone. Now the revolutionary was back.

"Maximilian's treasury," she said. "We must find it. As we agreed yesterday, I will return tonight for your answer about whether you will help us or not."

"I *could* tell you now—"

"No," she said, holding up her hand, "I do not want to hear it now. I do not want what happened between us last night to influence your decision. I did not whore myself to you to get you to help us. This was . . . personal."

"All right, then," he said. "Tonight."

She stood there a moment, looking at him. He had the feeling the woman in her wanted to kiss him good-bye, but the revolutionary wouldn't let her. Finally she simply turned and left.

Clint lay back down on the sheets, which smelled of her and of their sex. It was a shame she didn't get to act like a woman more often, he thought, just before he drifted off to sleep.

A knock at his door awoke him. Had Rosa come back? No, it was more likely Pete Townsend this time.

He opened the door and saw Townsend standing there, looking as if he hadn't gotten much sleep.

"I couldn't find her," he said, coming into the room uninvited. Did he know Rosa well enough to be able to smell her in the room? Clint hoped not.

"You mean you haven't been to sleep?"

"No," Townsend said. "I'm worried about what happened to her."

"She went home for the night, Pete," Clint said, "to get some sleep like you should have done."

"Do you think so?"

"Yes."

"I thought she'd come back . . . you know, for . . . well, never mind." Townsend rubbed his face with his hands. "Did she say she'd be coming back tonight?"

"That's right."

"Okay, then," Townsend said. "I guess I better get some sleep."

"I think that's a good idea."

Townsend looked at the bed. Did he smell her? Could he tell that two people had been in it all night?

"I'm sorry I woke you," he said, then. "Look, will you wake me in a few hours?"

"What for?" Clint asked. "Sleep as long as you want, Pete. She's not coming back until tonight."

"Yeah, I guess you're right," he said. "I guess she has a lot to do, huh?"

"I guess so."

"It's not easy for a woman in a revolution, you know? They don't give her the respect they'd give a man."

"I'm sure it's tough."

"Ah, you don't want to hear this," Townsend said. He rubbed his hands over his face again.

"Pete?"

"What?"

"Get out!" Clint said. "Go get some sleep. I'd still like another hour or two myself."

"Yeah, you're right," Townsend said. "I'm sorry . . ."

He headed for the door.

"Stop apologizing," Clint said. "Just go get some sleep."

"You'll wake me if anything happens?"

"I'll wake you right away," Clint said, "but nothing's going to happen. Trust me. Just get some sleep."

"Okay," Townsend said, "okay. Good night . . . or good morning, I guess."

"Whatever," Clint said. "I'll see you later."

Townsend finally left and Clint closed the door, feeling all of the guilt he hadn't allowed himself to feel the night before.

THIRTY-ONE

Clint woke a couple of hours later, feeling a bit disoriented. Without meaning to he seemed to have gotten himself involved in a triangle with Townsend and the lovely Rosa. Rosa had seemed determined that all they would have together was the one night. He agreed and vowed that it would be so.

Of course, being around both of them would be tricky, since he wouldn't want Townsend to find out about what he and Rosa had shared. He also wondered when Rosa would tell Townsend that she did not share his feelings—certainly not until *after* they found what they were looking for . . . Maximilian's treasury.

He dressed and went down to the hotel dining room for breakfast. While he ate, he considered his options; but in the end, he had to give in to his curiosity. Was there a treasury? And if so, just how much wealth was in it? These were things he found he wanted to know. It had nothing to do with wanting to help the revolutionaries. Mexico was not his country, and he didn't care who the head of it was. He just wanted to find out if this treasury was real.

By the time he was finished with his breakfast he had his answer ready for Rosa. He was glad she had stopped him from giving his decision the night before, because it would not have been the same one.

He walked through the lobby to the front doors and stepped outside. His curiosity stretched beyond the treasury, of course. He wanted to know who had sent the two men to kill him and Townsend yesterday. To his chagrin he realized that he had never even broached the subject with Rosa the night before. He would have been interested in seeing her reaction. Of course, after meeting her he no longer entertained the thought that she had sent the men. He truly believed that she wanted his help in finding the treasury. Still, she might have some idea about who had been behind the attempt. He would ask her about it when he saw her again.

It was too early to wake Townsend. He stared out at the square in front of the hotel, which was already teeming with people going about their business. Did he dare walk out among them? Was there someone out there waiting for another chance at him?

He decided he would chance it. In fact, he decided to go back to the place where they'd been attacked the day before. He wanted to ask that barber some questions.

It took him a few wrong turns but he finally found the street the shop was on. When he walked through the front door the barber, who was working on someone, took one look at him and tried to run. Unfortunately for him he was elderly and in no condition to run. Clint took two quick steps and caught the man by the back of the collar.

"Please, señor, please," the barber cried, covering his head with shaking hands, "*por favor*, do not kill me."

"I'm not here to kill you," Clint said, shaking the man by the collar. "Stop blubbering."

The man peeked at Clint from between his hands.

"You are not going to kill me?"

"No," Clint said, releasing his hold on the man, "I just want to ask you some questions."

"A-all right, señor," the barber said, "I will answer your questions."

"I want to know about the two men who tried to kill me and my friend yesterday."

"The *rurales* came and took them away after you left," the barber said.

"Did you tell them about us?"

"No, no, señor," the man said. "I told them nothing."

"Who were the two men?"

"I do not know."

"What did they say when they came in?"

"They asked where you were," the man said, "and then they told me to leave or they would kill me, too. I am sorry, señor, I am not a brave man—"

"That's all right, friend," Clint said. "I wouldn't expect you to go against two men with shotguns for me, a stranger."

"*Gracias*, señor."

"This is important, now."

The smaller man stood straight and said, "*Sí*, señor, I will help if I can."

"Did you ever see those men before?"

"No, señor, I am sorry. I wish I could help you—"

"Did either of them call the other by a name?"

The old man brightened and said, "*Sí*, I did hear a name. One called the other—*madre de Dios,* what is wrong with my memory." The old barber slammed the heels of his hands into his head.

"Take your time," Clint said. "Just think a moment."

"*Sí, sí,*" the man said, "I will take a moment—yes, yes, I remember. He called him Luis ... that was it! Luis."

A common name, Clint thought, which probably would be no help at all.

"All right, my friend," he said, "all right. Thank you."

The man shrugged and said, "I wish I could do more, señor."

"You have done enough. I won't bother you again."

As Clint left, the barber looked at the man in his chair, shrugged, and made the sign of the cross.

Clint headed back to the hotel. The streets were even more crowded than before, and he found himself looking forward to siesta time, when they would empty out. This way, stranger, friend, and foe looked alike. What was to keep someone from slipping right up behind him and sticking a knife or a gun in his ribs? He'd never even know what was happening until—

Suddenly, there it was, and for a moment he thought he was imagining it; but then whatever it was that was sticking him in the ribs pressed harder. A gun, he realized with relief, not a knife.

He stopped walking.

"*Hola*, Señor Gunsmith," a voice said in his ear.

"What do you want?"

"You have two choices, señor," the voice said.

"What are they?"

"You can die . . ."

"I don't like that one."

". . . or you can come with me."

"Let's go with the second one."

"*Bueno,*" the man said. "A good choice."

"Do you want my gun?"

"No, señor," the man said, and the gun in his ribs disappeared. "I do not want to shoot you, or be shot by you. I am but a messenger. Someone would like to see you."

"What was that business about two choices?" Clint asked.

The man laughed and said, "A game, señor. Forgive

me, please. I simply wanted to see how the great Gunsmith would react.''

Clint turned now and looked at the man. He was an
inch or two shorter, a swarthy but handsome man in his
thirties with a big black mustache. They were both being
jostled by the people walking by.

''What if I now choose not to go with you?''

The man shrugged and said, ''That would be your
choice, señor. I was only instructed to ask you to come
with me to talk about Maximilian's treasury.''

''The treasury?''

''*Sí*, señor,'' the man said. ''Will you come?''

''Lead the way.''

''My name is Carlos,'' the man said. ''Carlos Augusto
Velez-Colon, at your service, señor.''

''Carlos,'' Clint said, ''you wouldn't happen to know
a man named Luis, would you?''

A crafty look came into the man's eyes, and he said,
''I know many men named Luis, señor.''

''Like I said, Carlos,'' Clint repeated, ''lead the
way.''

THIRTY-TWO

Clint followed Carlos down a succession of streets and alleys, deciding that the man wasn't leading him into a trap. If he'd wanted to kill him he could have done so on the busy street, where no one would have noticed the body until they had to step over it.

No, apparently there actually was someone who wanted to talk to Clint about Maximilian's treasury, which had become one of his favorite subjects.

"How much longer, Carlos?" he asked.

"Not much further, señor."

Carlos wore a handgun and had bandoliers of cartridges crisscrossed over his torso. The very picture of a *bandido*.

"Here, just down this street."

It wasn't wide enough to be a street, but it wasn't narrow enough to be an alley. Carlos led Clint to a wooden door in the side of a stone building, knocked, waited, then knocked again. The door opened.

"This way, señor."

Clint wondered if they were going to go down into some more catacombs, as he had done with Rosa, but they remained on the street level until they reached a room with a desk as the only furniture. Behind the desk sat a man, dressed similarly to Carlos, but much larger and about ten years older.

"Here is here, *jefe*," Carlos said. "The Gunsmith."

The man looked up from the desk and showed Clint a mouthful of gold teeth.

"*Muy bien*, Carlos," he said, laughing. "I half expected to hear word that you were dead, but here you have brought him to me."

"It was not hard, *jefe*," Carlos said. "As you yourself said, as soon as he heard me mention Maximilian's treasury he was anxious to come."

"That is good. Carlos, go and get a chair for Señor Adams."

"That's okay," Clint said. "If nobody minds, I'll stand."

"Mmmm," the man said, "then you'll stand. Carlos, time for you to go."

"But . . . can you trust him?" Carlos asked. "Shall I take his gun from him?"

"I don't know. Can Carlos take your gun, señor?" the man asked.

"Not unless I want him to," Clint said.

The older man looked at Carlos and said, "Go."

"But *jefe*—"

"*Andale!*"

Carlos fell silent and grudgingly left the room.

"Señor Adams," the man said, "I hope that Carlos did not make this sound like anything more than a friendly invitation."

"He tried scaring the gringo," Clint said. "I can't blame him for that. Who are you, please?"

"You do not recognize me?"

"Sorry, no, I don't," Clint said. "Should I? Are you famous?"

"No, no," the man said, "not at all, señor. In fact, I prefer to go unrecognized, and to that end I will not introduce myself—if you don't mind?"

"I don't mind," Clint said, "but I would like to know why I was asked here."

"*Sí*, señor," the man said. "I will come to the point. Maximilian's treasury."

"I'm afraid that will only work once, my friend. If you don't have anything more for me than that I'll have to be—"

"I want to find it."

"What's that got to do with me?"

"I understand that you intend to find it."

"What makes you think that?"

"Please, señor, no games," the man said. "I know you have seen certain people who are looking for the treasury. I know that an offer has been made to you for your help. What I would like to know is if you are going to accept the offer."

"What's it to you?"

"Well, if you are still open for offers for your services I might be willing to, uh, make a bid."

"Sorry," Clint said, "I'm afraid my services aren't for sale."

"To anyone?"

"To anyone."

The man frowned.

"I do not think I understand. Does this mean you have no interest in finding Maximilian's treasury?"

"It means," Clint said, "that I can't be bought."

"Ah . . . but what if I was a beautiful señorita?" the man asked. "Could you be bought then?"

"Not unless you shaved first."

The man rubbed the stubble on his face and began to laugh.

"You are a funny man, señor," he said, finally. "I can be a funny man, too. I can be funny, or I can be dangerous. I am afraid the choice is yours."

"Is that a threat?"

"I do not make threats, señor," the man said. "I am

not a rattlesnake. I do not warn my prey before I strike.''

"Well," Clint said, "since you don't threaten, I guess I should take that as some friendly advice.''

The man thought for a moment, then nodded and said, "*Sí*, señor, that is good. Take it as friendly advice.''

"Okay, then," Clint said. "Is it all right if I go now?''

"*Sí*, señor, you may go. I will leave you to find your own way, if you do not mind. Carlos, he considers himself—how do you say in your country—a *pistolero*? I would not want him to be tempted by your very great reputation.''

"That's all right," Clint said. "I can find my way back.''

He backed away from the desk toward the doorway, eyes locked with those of the man behind the desk, ears cocked for any sound behind him.

"One thing before I go," he said, when he reached the doorway.

"Señor?''

"Do you know a man named Luis?''

"This is Mexico, señor," the man said. "I know many men named Luis.''

"That's what I was afraid of," Clint said, stepping into the darkened hallway.

THIRTY-THREE

When Clint got back to the hotel he went right to Townsend's room and knocked on the door. When there was no answer he knocked again, harder. He was about to give up when it opened. Townsend stared at him, but didn't look sleepy at all. In fact, he looked kind of pleased with himself.

"Can't you take a hint?" he asked Clint, a lopsided grin on his face.

"I thought I was supposed to wake you up."

"Well, somebody beat you to it."

Clint tried to look past Townsend to see who was in the room with him, but he couldn't see the bed from where he was. It was obviously a woman. He wondered if it was Rosa.

"Look, we have to talk—"

"Later," Townsend said, "we can talk later."

"No, now," Clint said. "It's about Maximilian's treasury."

"What about it?"

"Somebody else is interested in it."

"Who?"

"I don't know his name," Clint said, "but I just came from a meeting with him."

Townsend looked over his shoulder at whoever was in the room with him, then turned back to Clint and said, "Wait for me in the lobby. I'll be right down."

"I'll be in the dining room," Clint said. "I need some coffee."

"Fine," Townsend said. "Ten minutes."

"All right."

Clint moved slightly away from the door, but stayed in position to try and see through the crack between the door and the hinges as Townsend was closing the door. For a split second he got a look at the bed; the dark-haired, naked woman on it could have been Rosa—but it also could have been Carmalita or Carmen from Two Beers or any other dark-haired Mexican woman.

He waited still longer to see what he could hear. There was a murmur of voices, but he couldn't make out any of the words.

He went downstairs to wait for his friend.

THIRTY-FOUR

Clint sat at a table in the dining room that afforded him a view of the lobby. It paid off because when Townsend came down he was with the woman who had been in his bed. Clint watched as they exchanged a few words, then the woman kissed him and walked away.

The woman was Rosa.

Clint wondered what she was trying to pull. First she sleeps with him, telling him that there was nothing between her and Townsend; and now he finds her sleeping with Townsend. The woman had something on her mind, but what was it?

As Townsend approached the table and sat opposite him, Clint said, "You should have asked her to join us. She'd be interested in hearing this."

"Oh, you saw her."

"Everyone saw her, Pete," Clint said. "I thought she was trying to stay out of sight."

"She is," Townsend said. "She came by just a little after I went to bed and, well . . ."

"Never mind that now," Clint said. "I just had an interesting talk with a man who wouldn't give me his name."

"About what?"

"Maximilian's treasury."

"So someone else *is* lookin' for it."

"Definitely," Clint said. "And he tried to hire me to help him."

"And he didn't say who he was?"

"No, but I found out something else." He told Townsend about the talk he had with the barber, and of learning the name "Luis."

"And did you approach this fella with that name?"

"Yes," Clint said. "He and his helper said there are lots of Luises in Mexico, but how many Carlos Augusto Velez-Colons are there?"

"I give up," Townsend said. "How many?"

"Just one, I'll bet, and he fancies himself a *pistolero*, so somebody might know who he is and who he works for."

"Somebody like Rosa?"

"Maybe."

"I'll ask her," Townsend said. "She's coming back tonight."

"I know," Clint said. "For my answer."

"And what's your answer gonna be?"

"Well, even before I was taken to this fella today— Carlos called him *el jefe*—I had decided to go along for the ride and see if there really is a Maximilian's treasury."

"And did talkin' to this *el jefe* change your mind?" Townsend asked.

"No," Clint said, "it just made me more determined."

"Good," Townsend said. "Rosa will be glad to hear that from you. She has a lot of respect for you."

Clint poured himself a cup of coffee.

"You don't like her, do you?"

"I don't know her," Clint said evasively.

"Well, maybe you'll get to know her, now," Townsend said.

"Maybe."

"Do you think this *el jefe* is the man who sent those two to kill us?"

"No," Clint said. "Carlos Velez-Colon could have easily killed me today, and he didn't."

"Maybe he just changed his mind about having you killed," Townsend said. "Maybe he decided it was smarter to try to recruit you."

"Well, he tried and failed," Clint said. "Now we'll see if he goes back to wanting to have me killed."

"If you give Rosa her answer tonight she'll probably want to get started tomorrow."

"I assume she has a general idea of where this treasury might be?"

"Well, Maximilian was executed in Queretaro," Townsend said. "She thinks it will be somewhere around there."

"So she'll want to head for Queretaro," Clint said. "How many men will she have?"

"Well, counting us, her, and Manuel," Townsend said, "four."

"Only four?" Clint asked. "I thought she'd have this band of revolutionaries with her."

"She won't have a band of revolutionaries until she has Maximilian's treasury," Townsend said. "The men won't go with her until they know they can be armed."

"Wait a minute," Clint said. "She's spearheading this whole revolution?"

"She's trying to rally the forces."

"And the men will follow a woman?"

"They'll follow her."

That wasn't what she had indicated to Clint during their night together. She'd indicated to him that she was *only* a woman.

"Pete, do you know who she's trying to put into power?" Clint asked.

"No," Townsend said, "she won't say, not until they

have their army. She doesn't want to mention his name. She's afraid he'll be killed before they can put him in the palace. Why? Does that matter to you?''

"I'm just curious, that's all," Clint said.

Actually, he was wondering if Rosa had herself in mind for the job, which would explain why she was having a hard time raising an army.

"You can ask her tonight," Townsend said, "but I don't think she'll tell you."

"That's okay," Clint said. "For my part in all this, I really don't need to know."

THIRTY-FIVE

Townsend went back to his room after they talked, because he still had not had very much sleep. Clint didn't know what he should do at that point, so he went back to his room as well. He was surprised later when he woke up, because he did not even remember lying down. He looked up at the bedpost. At least he had remembered to hang his gun there before falling asleep. He also realized that he had slept through siesta. It seemed that it was contagious.

He got up and washed his face. Maybe he was getting to that age where he should just pick a place and settle down and hope people would start to forget. As long as he traveled around, his legend would never die, and there would always be somebody wanting to take a shot at him, for one reason or another.

But he wasn't at that age, yet. He liked being in the saddle. Maybe he'd just continue riding as long as Duke was able to carry him. They were both getting a little long in the tooth, but they each still had a lot of piss and vinegar left.

In the dining room with Townsend he'd only had coffee. Now he found that he was hungry, so he went down again. The same waiter sat him at the same table, but

139

he didn't say a word about having seen him just a little while ago.

"This time," he said to the waiter, "I think I'm going to eat."

"*Sí*, señor," the waiter said, "whatever you wish."

"Is your cook a good one?"

"*Sí*, he is very good."

"Then bring me whatever he suggests."

"*Sí*, señor," the waiter said, executing a slight bow, "as you wish."

It turned out to be a dish with chicken, rice, and what looked like fried bananas, and it was delicious. He was pleasantly surprised to find out there *were* bananas in it, and while they tasted like bananas, they also tasted like nothing he'd ever had before.

Afterward he ordered a pot of coffee and asked the waiter to tell the cook how much he enjoyed the food.

"*Sí*, señor," the man said, "I will tell him."

Clint was drinking his coffee when a man in uniform walked into the dining room. His uniform was very handsome, gray with silver trim. There was also a wide sombrero, which had been pushed back. He was wearing a sidearm in a flapped holster and a saber.

"*Rurales*," the waiter said. Clint hadn't even realized that the man had approached the table.

"What rank is he?" Clint asked.

"*Capitan*."

What was a captain in the *rurales* doing here? Was he going to eat, or was he looking for someone?

In that moment Clint realized that the man was looking for him—and their eyes met.

"I think you better bring another cup," Clint said to the waiter, as the captain started toward him.

"*Sí*, señor."

The waiter moved away, and the captain approached. Clint realized that the uniform looked better from a distance. Up close it looked stiff, and he realized it had not been washed in some time.

"Señor Adams?" the man asked. "Clint Adams?"

"That's right," Clint said. "What can I do for you, Captain?"

"I am Capitan Esteban Romero y DeJesus, señor," the soldier said. "I may sit?"

"Yes, please," Clint said. "Have some coffee."

"*Gracias*, señor," he said, taking a seat. The waiter appeared at that moment with another cup, and Clint lifted the pot and filled it.

"Señor, you will please forgive my appearance, but I have been riding for some time."

"That's all right, Captain," Clint said. "There's never any need to apologize for doing your job."

The captain sipped the coffee and closed his eyes gratefully.

"This hotel makes very good coffee, no?"

"Yes, it does. Tell me, Captain, is there something I can help you with?"

"I hope so, señor," DeJesus said. "Two men were killed not far from here, in a barbershop."

"That's terrible," Clint said. "Today?"

"No, señor, yesterday."

"So why are you here today?"

"I have only just arrived back in the city today, señor, and my superiors assigned me to look into these killings."

"And why did that bring you here to me?"

"You are a very well-known American *pistolero*, señor."

"So when someone is killed you come to me? Were these men shot?"

"*Sí*, señor."

"Well, what can I tell you, Captain? Do you want to know if I shot them?"

"Would you tell me if you did?"

"I don't think so, Captain. I would not relish a visit to one of your Mexican prisons."

The captain made a face and said, "They are terrible places." He looked at the coffeepot very pointedly.

"Would you like another cup?" Clint asked.

"Oh, *sí*, thank you, señor. You are most kind."

"Captain," Clint said, as DeJesus sipped from the second cup, "how else may I help you?"

"You and another man went into this barbershop, with the baths in the back. You had haircuts, yes?"

Clint didn't answer.

"And baths?"

Clint still remained silent.

"Surely, señor," the captain said, "you do not think I would charge you with a crime for having haircuts and baths?"

"All right," Clint said, "we did. Was it in this same shop that the bodies were found?"

"Oh, *sí*, señor."

"Then it must have happened after we left."

The captain sat back and flapped his arms, as if he was a dunce for not having thought of that himself.

"Of course!" he said happily. "It happened after you left."

Clint waited for the next question, wondering if the old man at the barbershop had given them away to the *rurales*.

"Señor, when you left the barbershop, did you see anyone else there?"

"No," Clint said, "not anyone. In fact, when we left the barber was not even there."

"I see," DeJesus said. He finished his coffee and put the cup down. "Excellent coffee. Well, Señor Adams, I have taken up enough of your time."

The man stood up.

"I hope you find your killers, Captain."

"I hope so, too, señor," DeJesus said. "My superiors

do not tolerate failure. Thank you for the coffee.''

"You're welcome.''

The captain inclined his head slightly, then turned and walked out of the dining room. Clint realized that they had been the center of attention. Now that the captain had left, everyone was staring at Clint, obviously wondering who he was and what he had done.

And, probably, why he was not on his way to prison.

THIRTY-SIX

"Señor?" the waiter asked.

"Yes?"

"You have broken the law?"

"I don't think so," Clint said. "If I had he would have taken me away, no?"

"Perhaps," the waiter said, with a shrug. "Señor, a man gave me a peso to tell you that he would meet you behind the hotel."

"What man?"

"I do not know. He came into the kitchen."

"And where is he now?"

"He went out the back door. He said he would be waiting there."

"What did he look like?"

"What do they all look like, señor?" the waiter said. "A *bandido*."

"I see."

"You can go through the kitchen and out the back door, señor."

"Was this man alone?"

"*Sí*, señor, he was very alone."

"What's your name?"

"Domingo."

"Well, thank you, Domingo. I think I'll pay my bill and go and see what the man wants."

"*Sí*, señor."

Clint did just that and then followed Domingo through the kitchen to the back door.

"Thank you, Domingo."

"*De nada,*" the man said.

Clint stepped outside.

"Señor," Carlos Augusto Velez-Colon said, "how wonderful of you to come."

"The invitation could only have come from you, Carlos," Clint said. "Does your *jefe* want to see me again?"

"No, señor," Carlos said, dropping a cigarette to the ground and stepping on it. "He simply sent me with a message for you."

"And what would that be?"

"He wants you to know that if you have trouble with the *rurales*, he can probably be of some assistance to you."

"What kind of assistance, Carlos?"

"He has—how do you gringos say it?—ah, he has the connections."

"I see. And what makes him think I might be in trouble with the *rurales*?"

"I think you must be, señor, or why would a captain of the *rurales* have come to the hotel looking for you, eh?"

"But how would your boss know that unless he sent the captain?"

Carlos frowned.

"Tell your boss it's not going to work, Carlos," Clint said.

"What will not work?"

Clint wondered if Carlos realized that his boss had sent the captain to try and scare Clint into working for him. Did he even know that his boss had those kinds of connections?

"Just tell him, Carlos," Clint said. "That's my message to him. It's not going to work."

"I will tell him," Carlos said, "but I do not think it will make him happy."

"That's too bad," Clint said, "but making him happy is your job; it sure ain't mine."

Carlos looked undecided about what to do.

"That's it, Carlos," Clint said. "We're done."

Clint reached for the back door to go back into the hotel through the kitchen, but it was locked. The two men ended up having to walk down an alley together to get to the street, and they did so in silence.

When they reached the street, Clint stood there and watched Carlos walk away. If *el jefe* had connected with the *rurales*, Clint decided that he and Townsend should probably switch hotels.

Or get out of town.

THIRTY-SEVEN

As Clint was going upstairs to wake Townsend—again—
he realized that while Captain DeJesus had known there
were two of them at the barbershop, he'd never mentioned Townsend's name. Which meant that he either
knew it already or didn't care. Either way, it was a bad
situation.

He banged on Townsend's door until the man opened
it, bleary-eyed.

"What the—" he started, but Clint didn't give him a
chance to go any further.

"Never mind," he said. "Get your stuff together. We
have to get out of here."

"Wha-what?"

"Do you trust me, Pete?"

"Of course I trust you, but—"

"Then get your gear together, and I'll explain it all
to you on the way."

Clint turned and went into his own room to pack his
saddlebags. He grabbed his rifle and went back into the
hall. Townsend was coming out of his room, looking
disheveled, but carrying his things.

"Come on," Clint said, and started down the hall.

"What's goin' on?" Townsend asked, following.

"I just had a visit from a captain of the *rurales*."

"What?"

"He asked about those two men we killed."

"He knew?"

"I think so."

"Why didn't he arrest you?"

"Because he was sent to scare me."

"Scare you? Why?"

"To try to get me to work for that *el jefe* fella."

"He sent the *rurales* after you? How do you know that?"

"Because his *pistolero* just about told me so afterward," Clint said. "Said his boss had connections and could help if we got in trouble with the *rurales*."

They headed down the steps, but before they reached the bottom Clint saw Captain DeJesus enter the lobby with about half a dozen *rurales* behind him, all holding their rifles like they meant business.

"Up, up," he whispered to Townsend. "Go back up!"

They returned to the second floor before they were seen.

"Now they're coming to arrest us," Clint said. "We've got to find a back way."

They moved down to the end of the hall and found only a window. There was, however, a panel in the ceiling.

"The roof," Clint said.

"We could be trapped up there," Townsend pointed out.

"We're going to be trapped right here if we don't do something."

"Okay, boost me," Townsend said, dropping his gear.

Clint linked his hands and gave Townsend a leg up. The man moved the panel in the ceiling and climbed through. Clint handed up his and Townsend's gear; then he jumped up, grabbed Townsend's arm, and allowed himself to be pulled up through the panel as footsteps sounded on the stairs.

"Get that panel back in place," he ordered his friend. "They're coming."

They looked around the roof, which was wide and empty at the moment.

"How long before they look up here?" Townsend asked.

"Who knows?" Clint asked. "Check that side; I'll check over here. We've got to find a way down."

Clint went over to his side but there was no way down, just a sheer drop. The front wasn't an option. He didn't even want to look down for fear he'd see a whole garrison of *rurales* waiting for them. He started for the back, but Townsend called him over.

"There's another roof," he said.

"How far?"

Clint joined Townsend on his side and saw that it was pretty far, and about ten feet lower.

"It's our only chance," Townsend said, "but we could easily break a leg."

"Or miss," Clint said.

"I'll go first," Townsend said.

"Why should you go first?"

"I'm younger."

"I have longer legs."

"When I get there you can toss the rifles and the saddlebags over to me."

"Forget the saddlebags," Clint said. "There's nothing in them we can't replace, but you're right about the rifles."

"See? You're better than me with guns."

"Shooting them," Clint reminded him, "not throwing them."

"The longer we argue the more chance there is they'll look up here," Townsend said. "I'll go first."

"All right," Clint said. "You go first."

Townsend nodded and handed Clint his rifle.

"Better take a running start," Clint said.

"Right."

"And don't make any noise on the way, uh, down."

Townsend backed up, took a few deep breaths, then ran toward the edge of the roof . . . and jumped off.

THIRTY-EIGHT

Clint saw Townsend disappear beneath the edge of the roof. He waited for a thud of some kind, but instead heard a sort of skidding sound. He ran to the edge, prepared to see Townsend's body lying in the alley. Instead, Townsend was getting to his feet on the other roof, looking at his hands and his knees.

"You all right?" Clint called, but not too loudly in case there were *rurales* in front of the hotel.

"Skinned my hands and my knees, but I'm okay," he said. "Toss the rifles over."

Clint threw one rifle and then the other over to Townsend, who deftly caught them.

"Now jump; it's easier than it looks. I jumped too hard."

Clint looked down, then turned and walked back to where Townsend had started. He didn't care if Townsend *had* jumped too hard; he'd made it, and that was what counted. He took a breath and then ran toward the end of the roof and jumped.

Once they were on the lower roof it was easy to find their way down. They were able to drop to another roof

153

next door, and from there to the ground. What they found there surprised them.

"I thought they were going to catch you," Rosa said to them.

Both of them wheeled around, crouching, at the sound of her voice, and then straightened when they saw it was her.

"How did you get here?" Clint asked.

"I was coming to see you when I saw the *rurales* going inside," she said. "What happened?"

"Clint says—" Townsend began.

"We can talk about that when we're safe somewhere," Clint said.

"All right, then," Rosa said, "come on."

She was wearing a sombrero and a man's shirt and pants. She started off down the alley, and Clint and Townsend followed.

"Are you going to that church?" Clint asked.

"No," she said, "somewhere else."

"Why don't we just go and get our horses?" Clint suggested.

She stopped, turned, and looked at him.

"You agree to help us?"

"Yes," Clint said, "and I think we should get going as soon as possible."

"I agree," she said. "Yes, all right, we will go and get your horses, and then collect Manuel and be on our way."

"Only Manuel?" Clint asked. "No other men?"

"Only Manuel," she said, "until later."

"Okay," Clint said, "then lead the way . . ."

They approached the livery carefully. Clint didn't know if anyone knew where they were keeping their horses. He hadn't explained anything to Rosa yet, about the man he only knew as *el jefe*, or about Carlos the *pistolero* or

Captain DeJesus, because he wanted to watch her face when he did.

"Looks clear," he said. "Rosa, wait here and we'll get the horses."

She nodded and kept watch while they went inside and saddled their mounts. They had left their saddlebags on the rooftop, but it would be up to Rosa to get them supplies for their trip. Maybe she could get them some saddlebags, too—and a couple of spare shirts.

They walked their horses out and mounted up. Townsend reached down to pull Rosa up behind him but she declined his hand and walked over to Clint, saying, "Clint has a stronger horse."

That was not something Townsend could legitimately argue, although he looked like he wanted to.

Clint lifted Rosa up behind him, and she wrapped her arms around his midsection and crushed her breasts against his back. Clint could feel Pete Townsend's eyes fastened on them.

"Loosen up," he said to her. "You're going to cut me in half."

"I did not think you would mind," she said, but she loosened her hold a bit.

"Play your games some other time, Rosa," he said. "For now just direct us which way to go."

"All right," she said, and pointed. "That way. We will have to stay off main streets if the *rurales* are looking for you."

"Good idea."

"And when we get where we are going you will have to tell me why the *rurales* are looking for you."

"Don't worry," Clint said, "I'll tell you."

"Hey, are we going?" Townsend asked, sounding annoyed.

"We're going," Clint said, and headed Duke off in the direction Rosa was pointing.

THIRTY-NINE

Rosa directed them to a run-down section of town where the people they rode by kept their heads down and did not even look at them.

"What's wrong with them?" Townsend asked.

"When they are questioned," she replied, "they want to be able to say they saw nothing."

"Why would they expect to be questioned?"

"They always expect to be questioned."

She called their progress to a halt in front of a small, rickety shack. They dismounted and she said, "Wait here."

She went inside and came out with Manuel. Following them was a woman holding a baby. Rosa came over to stand by Clint and Townsend while Manuel spoke with the woman, who was visibly upset. She was in her thirties and was by no means pretty, and she kept directing hot, hostile glances toward Rosa.

"His wife?" Townsend asked.

"Yes, and their baby," Rosa replied.

"She doesn't like you," Clint said.

"No."

"Is she jealous?"

"No," she said, in a different tone. "It is not as a

157

woman she dislikes me. She knows I am no threat to
her that way. Manuel loves her dearly, and the baby.''

"Then why—" Townsend started.

"Because I am taking him away to fight," she said.
"Consuelo does not believe in revolution."

"This revolution?" Clint asked. "Or any?"

"Any," Rosa said. "She has seen several, and she
says that nothing ever changes. One tyrant, one dictator
is the same as another."

"Sounds like a smart woman," Clint said.

"Sounds like your country's democracy, yes?" Rosa
replied.

"Where are your horses?" Clint asked.

"Behind the house."

"Wait here," Clint said. "Pete and I will saddle them
for you."

"*Gracias.*"

Townsend and Clint rode around to the back of the
house where they found two horses under a lean-to.
They each took one and saddled it.

"This one is Rosa's," Townsend said of the bay he
was saddling.

"Fine."

"What was that about democracy?" Townsend asked.

"What?"

"Democracy," Townsend repeated. "Rosa mentioned
something about it."

"Must have been something I said to her."

"Oh," Townsend said, and then added, "When?"

"Probably when we were talking without you."

"You told her you don't approve of revolution?"

"No," Clint said. "I think I said that in our country
one politician was pretty much as good or bad as another, and if we didn't like one we didn't kill him, we
just voted him out."

"Uh-huh," Townsend said, and then added, "Like
Lincoln?"

"That was still wartime thinking," Clint said, "by a fanatic who thought he was going to reverse the outcome with one shot."

They finished saddling the horses and walked them around to the front. Manuel was holding the woman in his arms, and she was weeping.

"Any chance she'll be able to talk him out of coming with us?" Townsend asked.

"None," Rosa said, without hesitation. "Manuel is loyal."

Clint wondered if she meant that the man was loyal to Mexico or to her.

"I am ready," Manuel said, approaching them. Clint handed the man the reins of his horse. *"Gracias."*

Clint said, *"De nada,"* because that was what Domingo the waiter had said to him.

Now they stood for a moment, each with his own horse. The woman had withdrawn into the house, and they could hear the baby crying.

"Tell me about the *rurales*," Rosa said.

Clint explained that Captain DeJesus had visited him earlier, in the dining room, to talk about the two men he and Townsend had killed.

"How did he know about that?" Rosa asked.

"Simple," Clint said. "Somebody told him."

"Who?"

"I have an idea."

"Who?" Manuel asked.

"Do either of you know a man named Carlos Augusto Velez-Colon?"

"Son of a *puta*," Manuel said, and spat.

"We know Carlos," Rosa said.

"Do you know who he works for?"

"Anyone who will pay him," Rosa said.

"Well, he's working for some guy he calls *el jefe*," Clint said.

"Carlos calls everyone he works for *el jefe*," Rosa said.

"Well, this *el jefe* is in his forties, thickly built with a mouthful of gold teeth."

Clint thought he saw a flicker of recognition in Manuel's eyes—and a warning from Rosa to him by a movement of *her* eyes.

"Does that sound familiar?" Clint asked.

"It sounds like a lot of men," Rosa said. "If this one sent the *rurales* after you, he must have some connections with them—or with Captain DeJesus."

"Do you know him, too?" Clint asked.

"We know of him," she said. "If he is after you, we should put as many miles between him and us as possible."

"Why?" Townsend asked.

"Because he is not a man who gives up," she said. "If he is after you, for whatever reason, he will keep coming until he catches you—or until he is dead."

"Even if the order didn't come from his superiors?" Clint asked.

"If he is working for this *el jefe* of yours," Rosa said, "then he thinks of him as his superior."

"So where are we going?" Townsend asked.

"We will go to the place Maximilian was last seen," Rosa said, "the place where he was executed. We will go to Querétaro."

FORTY

They rode north. Rosa told them it would take several days to reach their destination. They stopped in the first town they came to and picked up basic supplies, but they traveled light so they wouldn't need any pack animals. That would make them too easy to track, too easy to catch up with.

They camped the first night and divvied up the chores. Manuel collected wood for the fire, Townsend and Clint took care of the horses. Rosa had agreed to cook for them, something Clint would not have suggested for fear she would rebel against being given a woman's job. In actuality, Clint thought of cooking on the trail as a man's job.

Rosa prepared some beans and bacon for them and coffee, which they all started with.

"Is your baby a boy or a girl?" Clint asked Manuel, as they waited for the food.

"A girl, señor," Manuel said. "Isobel."

"How old?"

"Only . . . how do you say . . . *quatro* . . ."

"Four months," Rosa said.

"*Sí,*" Manuel said, "four months. She is very beautiful, like her mother."

Clint had gotten a good look at Manuel's wife, and she could not have been called beautiful by any stretch of the imagination. However, he was sure that Manuel thought she was.

"I am going to free Mexico for her," Manuel said.

"That's an admirable goal, Manuel," Clint said. "We'd all like to see our country be free."

"Your country is free, señor."

"Sometimes I wonder."

"About what?" Manuel asked with a frown.

"Oh, whether a country is ever really free," Clint said. "It has to be governed by someone; someone has to make the laws in order for it to be civilized. But if a country is to be very civilized, I don't think it can really be free."

"I do not understand, señor," Manuel said. "You are not . . . ruled. You do not have a dictator."

"We have lawmakers," Clint said, "and if we break the law we have to pay. That is, in a way, being ruled."

"You are just confusing him," Rosa said, handing out plates of food. "You cannot compare Mexico to your country. You are free, we are not, and have not been for a very long time."

"I suppose not," Clint said.

"But that will all change very soon," Rosa said, sitting back with her own plate. "As soon as we find Maximilian's treasury we will be able to fund our revolution."

"There's someone else looking for the treasury, though."

"Who?"

"The man I told you about."

"*El jefe?*" Rosa said.

Again, he thought he saw her cast a warning glance Manuel's way.

"Yes. He tried to hire me to find it for him."

Rosa stopped with her fork halfway to her mouth and regarded Clint over her plate.

"But you refused."

"Of course I did."

"Because you are working for us."

"I'm not working *for* you," Clint said. "I'm working *with* you."

"What is the difference?" Manuel asked.

Clint turned his glance from Rosa to Manuel.

"I'm not being paid by you."

"You are not?" Manuel looked surprised.

"No," Clint said.

"We offered to pay—" Rosa started.

"I agreed to help," Clint said. "I did not ask to be paid."

"But this man, *el jefe*," Manuel said, "he offered to pay you?"

"Yes."

"And you would prefer to help us for nothing?"

"Yes."

Rosa and Manuel exchanged a glance, and then looked at Townsend.

"Don't look at me," he said. "I can't explain it."

FORTY-ONE

"That is Querétaro," Rosa said. They could see the town in the distance.

"It's not very big," Clint said.

"Once it was bigger," Rosa said, "and of much more importance."

"Well, once we get there how are we going to have any idea of where to look for Maximilian's treasury?" Clint asked.

"We are not going there," Rosa said.

"Why not?" Clint asked.

"Because he would not have hidden the treasury in the town," she said. "It would have been too dangerous."

"So you think he hid it somewhere out here?" Clint asked, looking across the plains. There didn't appear to be too many possible hiding places . . . unless he'd buried it.

"Wait a minute—"

"Pete," she said, "I need the map."

Townsend took the map from his shirt pocket and gave it to her.

"Wait a minute," Clint said. "That map is real?"

165

"Of course it's real," Townsend said. "Why else would she have given it to me?"

"But—"

"Shhh," Townsend said, "let's see what she says."

Clint frowned unhappily. If the map was real, why had she told him it wasn't? Was she afraid he was going to steal it? And if it *was* real and of such importance, why had she given it to Pete Townsend to carry around in his shirt pocket all this time?

"It's a good thing that map wasn't in the saddlebags we left on the roof of the hotel," Clint said to Townsend.

"It was," Townsend said. "I took it out before I jumped."

"We have to go that way," Rosa said, pointing.

Townsend reached out for the map, but Rosa passed it to Manuel without giving him a glance. She nudged her horse forward and they followed.

"Where'd she get the map, Pete?"

"She never said."

"Why didn't she give it back to you to hold?"

Townsend thought for a moment and then said, "Maybe because all of the writing on it is in Spanish."

"Yeah," Clint said, "maybe . . ."

Clint looked around, unable to shake the uncomfortable feeling that they were being watched—but from where? He also had the feeling that Rosa didn't need them at all to find the treasury. He thought she needed them—him—to protect it when they did find it.

And what would she need them for after that?

Rosa and Manuel rode together up ahead. More and more Clint felt a separation between the two of them and himself and Townsend.

"What's wrong?" Townsend asked.

"Why?"

"You look antsy."

"I feel antsy," Clint said. "Something's not right."

"Want to tell Rosa?"

"No," Clint said, "because the something that's not right might be her."

"What do you mean?" Townsend asked. "Are you starting to not trust her again?"

"I never did trust her, Pete."

"Why not?"

"Well," Clint said, "for one thing she told me the map she gave you was no good."

"What?" Townsend asked. "Why would she tell you a thing like that?"

"I don't know."

"Maybe she never trusted you."

"And what did she think I was going to do?" Clint asked. "Steal it from you?"

Rosa stopped abruptly, and Manuel gave her the map to look at again.

"Look," Clint said, leaning over so only Townsend could hear him, "just stay alert, okay?"

"Sure, Clint."

"No, I mean it," Clint said. "Be ready for anything, Pete."

"I said all right," Townsend said, but it wasn't the least bit comforting that he kicked his horse and trotted up to where Rosa was. She ignored him and continued to study the map, then handed it back to Manuel.

"This way," she said, and started off again.

Now the front three were abreast and Clint was bringing up the rear. He didn't like the feeling of isolation. He also didn't like it that at that moment he trusted no one to watch his back if things went bad.

All his life he'd thought that he would die one of two ways. Either shot in the back like Hickok, by someone too cowardly to face him, or shot because he had no one to watch his back when the lead started flying.

FORTY-TWO

"Do we know what we're looking for?" Townsend asked Rosa.

"It's buried."

"What?"

"It is buried," she said. "He buried it somewhere around here."

"According to your map?" Clint called out.

She turned in her saddle and looked at him.

"That's right."

"And where did you get that map?"

"It was given to me," she said, "by a dead man."

"Oh, well, then," Clint said, "it must be valid."

"It was given to me by a man I trusted," Rosa said, slowly, "on his deathbed. He swore to me that Maximilian's treasury was buried out here, and that the map would lead me to it."

"So then where is it?" Townsend asked. "You've been lookin' at that map for hours."

"It is near," she said, "very near."

With that she started her horse forward again, and the three men followed.

* * *

"There," Rosa said, but while Manuel and Townsend looked where she was pointing, Clint was looking behind them.

"Looks like a headstone," Townsend said.

"Dust cloud," Clint said.

"What?" Townsend asked.

"Behind us," Clint said. "A dust cloud. From the size of it there are a lot of riders coming."

"How long will it be before they reach us?" Rosa asked.

"Less than an hour."

"The headstone is our marker," she said, and started riding toward it.

When they reached the headstone, Rosa, Manuel, and Townsend dismounted. Clint stayed mounted so he could watch the dust cloud. As it turned out it wasn't a headstone, but a wooden marker in the shape of one.

"We have to dig it up," Rosa said.

"Is that a good idea?" Clint asked.

"Why not?" Townsend asked.

"Because we've got less than an hour," Clint said. "What if it's buried deep?"

"What do you suggest?" Rosa asked.

"If you're satisfied that this is the marker on your map, and that this is where the treasury is buried, you can always come back to it. I suggest we get out of here now and head for the town."

"And then what?" she asked.

"We can find out who these riders are if they stop."

"And if they do not stop?" she asked.

"Then they'll probably have ridden by and we can come back here."

Rosa looked at Manuel, who shrugged. She did not look to Townsend for advice. She stared down at the wooden headstone, biting her lip.

"They could be *rurales*," Clint said, "or they could

be *el jefe*'s men—only you know who *el jefe* really is, don't you, Rosa?''

''I do not know what you mean.''

''Sure you do,'' Clint said, but he didn't pursue it.

''This has to be the place,'' Townsend said. ''Why else would there be a marker here?''

''How about because somebody died and his friends or family decided to bury him right here?'' Clint suggested.

''I say we dig now,'' Townsend said, ''find out what's here.''

But nobody had asked him.

''All right,'' Rosa said, causing Townsend to think she was agreeing with him, but then she went on, ''we'll go to Querétaro.''

''What?'' Townsend asked.

''Clint is right.''

''But we're this close to it!'' Townsend said.

''And they're getting close to us,'' Clint said. ''If we start to dig they're going to catch us at it. If that happens we'll have nothing.''

Rosa said something to Manuel in Spanish. He hurriedly mounted and started riding hell bent for leather for Querétaro.

''Where's he going?'' Townsend asked.

''To have everything ready for us when we reach town,'' Rosa said. She walked to her horse and mounted. She and Clint looked down at Townsend.

''Are you coming?'' she asked him.

''Yeah, yeah,'' he said, walking toward his horse, ''I'm coming, but I want you to know that I don't agree with this decision.''

''We know that,'' she said. With that she wheeled her horse around and rode off in the direction Manuel had just gone.

Townsend took a last, longing look at the grave, then he and Clint followed her.

FORTY-THREE

When they rode into Querétaro, Rosa seemed to know exactly where she was going. She rode unwaveringly down the main street, which took them past the gallows from which Maximilian had been hanged.

This seemed to be all the town had, however. The streets seemed empty, and as far as Clint could figure, it was not siesta time. They rode past a hotel, which Rosa ignored, and past a livery, also ignored. She finally took them to a one-story adobe house, reining in right in front of it. As they dismounted Manuel came out.

"We can put the horses in the back," he said, and collected the reins of all three of their horses. Rosa led Clint and Townsend inside.

"Is this a ghost town?" Townsend asked.

"Not quite," she said.

The house was one large room with sleeping bags on the floor and a fire going in the fireplace. Suspended over the flames was a pot with something cooking in it, probably stew. Tortillas were flattened out on rocks in front of the fire.

"Rosa," Clint said, "somebody should be outside keeping a watch for the men I saw."

"Manuel will do it," she said. "I will tell him when he comes in."

When Manuel did come in, however, it was not under his own power. The door slammed open, and he came hurtling through, rolling to the floor. When he came to a stop they could see that he was bleeding from a scalp wound, probably the result of a pistol-whipping.

"Manuel—" Rosa said, rushing to him.

"In the house!" a voice called outside.

Clint and Townsend both drew their weapons. Clint looked quickly at Rosa, to see if she looked surprised. Was it possible she had led them into this trap?

"Hello in the house," the voice called. "Señor Adams, I know you are in there."

"Who—" Townsend said.

"It's that fella *el jefe*," Clint said.

"No," she said. "His name is Fernando Portillo."

"Portillo?" Clint said. "I don't know the name."

"You once asked me who I was fighting to put into power in Díaz's place."

"Portillo?"

"It *was* Portillo," she said, "but no more."

"Does he know that you're no longer working for him?" Clint asked.

She sighed and said, "He does now."

Manuel came to and told them that he had been jumped in the back when he went to care for the horses. Before being pistol-whipped he saw about six men, and recognized Portillo and Carlos Augusto Velez-Colon.

"Six," Clint said. "Is that all?"

"*Sí,*" Manuel said, holding his head. Portillo and his men were apparently so cocky they had not bothered to take Manuel's gun from him.

"What is it?" Townsend asked Clint.

"Well, six isn't enough to raise the dust I saw," Clint said, "so that means we're still expecting company."

"Maybe Portillo doesn't know," Townsend said. "If

it's *rurales*, and we can hold out long enough—''

"There's only one problem with that," Clint said.

"What?"

"If it's *rurales* we don't know if they're with Portillo or against him."

They looked at Rosa.

"You already know Portillo has connections," she said. "We will just have to wait and see."

"Señor Adams," Portillo shouted, "I grow impatient with this."

"What do you want, Portillo?"

There was a pause, as Portillo digested the fact that Clint knew his name.

"I want you to come out with your hands up," he said. "All of you."

"And then what?"

"And then you and your friend can go your way, señor," Portillo said. "You are Americans, and I suggest you go back to your country."

"And what happens to Rosa and Manuel?"

"That is not your concern."

"Clint," Townsend said, "if there's six of them we can take 'em."

"How do you figure that?"

"You take four, I'll take the other two."

"Your confidence is overwhelming."

"He is right, Clint," Rosa said. "You are, after all, a legend. If you step out there and face them, you will frighten them. Frightened men cannot shoot straight."

"Señor Adams!"

"I'm thinking it over!" Clint called back. He turned to Rosa. "I've got some questions for you, Rosa, and I want the truth. We may be moments from being shot, and I think you owe us that much."

"What do you want to know?"

"I want to know your game," Clint said. "You seem

to be telling me one thing and Pete another. Why is that?''

She shrugged.

''I had to keep you both interested.''

''What's goin' on?'' Townsend asked.

''She's been playing us, partner,'' Clint said. ''I don't think she ever meant to turn any of that treasury over to you.''

''Is that true?'' Townsend asked.

She shrugged.

''I thought you loved me.''

She laughed at that.

''You are not a man women can love, gringo,'' Rosa said. ''You have had many women. How many have you loved?''

''I could have loved you.''

''We will never know, then. As for me, I love my country.''

Townsend looked at Clint.

''Still want to risk your life for her and her revolution?''

''Not a chance,'' Townsend said.

''Portillo?'' Clint called. ''We're coming out!''

''What are you doing?'' Rosa demanded.

''What you said. We're going to step out there and see what happens.''

''Think they'll try to kill us?'' Townsend asked.

''They tried once,'' Clint said, ''but maybe we can convince them that we just want to go home. In any case, be ready.''

Townsend nodded.

''Wait—'' Rosa said.

''I suggest you stay inside for now, Rosa,'' Clint said. ''If he's reasonable, we can talk him into letting you come out safely.''

''Safely?'' she asked. ''And if he lets you leave, how long do you think he will keep us alive? He knows that the people will never follow him as long as I am alive."

"That's pretty funny, Rosa," Clint said.

"What is?"

"Well," he said, "the people don't seem so ready to follow you now, either. Are you sure they even want a revolution?"

Before she could answer, Clint opened the door and stepped out.

FORTY-FOUR

Once he was out, Clint moved to one side. Townsend stepped out after him and moved to the other side. They waited.

Fernando Portillo was sitting on his horse, at the center of a line formed by him and his men. Next to him was Carlos Velez-Colon.

"What now, Portillo?" Clint asked.

"It is up to you, señor," Portillo replied. "How involved do you want to be with my country's politics?"

"Not at all."

"And with Maximilian's treasury?"

"The same."

"And your friend?"

Townsend answered for himself. "I just want to get out of here alive."

"Muy bien," Portillo said. "I suggest you both get on your horses and ride north."

"That's it?" Clint asked.

"Sí," Portillo replied, "that is, as you say, it."

But Clint couldn't leave it at that.

"What about Rosa and Manuel?"

"Señor, if I wanted them dead the man would have been thrown into the house already dead."

179

That made sense to Clint.

"Let's go, Clint," Townsend said. "It ain't our fight."

"Now you think of that?" Clint muttered.

"Better late than never," Townsend said.

"Go around the house that way," Portillo said, pointing to Clint's right.

"Come on, Pete."

Clint moved sideways, followed by Townsend, both of them keeping their eyes on the men. When they reached the end of the wall they turned and hurried around to the back. Their horses were still saddled. Apparently, Portillo and his men had gotten to Manuel before he could unsaddle them.

"Do you think he'll kill Rosa?" Townsend asked.

"I don't know," Clint said. "If he does and any of the people are loyal to her, he'll make a martyr out of her."

They were about to mount up when a voice said, "Señor! I do not think I want you to go."

Clint turned and saw Carlos Velez-Colon standing there with three other men.

"Your boss said we could go, Carlos."

"*I* did not say you could go," Carlos said. "Come, we will see who is faster."

"At two-to-one odds?" Clint asked.

Carlos shrugged.

"After all, señor, you *are* a legend."

With that the man drew—or tried to. Clint drilled him in the center of the chest before he could clear leather. Townsend pulled his gun, slower than Clint, but as accurately, and shot one of the other men. The remaining two men ran.

"Think Portillo sent them?" Townsend asked.

"He had to know."

"What do we do now?"

"We've got to ride past him to get out," Clint said.

"Let's do it, then."

They mounted up and rode around the bodies. When they got to the front Portillo was still on his horse, but his men had gone inside. He and Clint exchanged an expressionless glance, and then Clint and Townsend rode off down the street.

When they reached the end of town, they saw the riders coming toward them. A full complement of *rurales*, led by Captain Esteban DeJesus.

"Shit," Townsend said.

"Sit tight," Clint said. "They don't want us."

The *rurales* continued toward them at a gallop, while Clint and Townsend were moving at a trot. At the last minute they moved aside to allow the men to get by. DeJesus' eyes met Clint's, and there was just a flicker of recognition.

"Jesus," Townsend said, "why'd they just go by us without stopping?"

"We're American," Clint said.

"In that case," Townsend said, "let's get back to where we came from."

It was at Townsend's insistence, though, that they rode back the way they had come, to the grave marked with a wooden headstone. When they got there, there was nothing but a big empty hole.

"Goddamn it!" Townsend said. "It was there."

"Maybe," Clint said.

"You think they dug it up and found it empty?"

Clint, staring into the grave, said again, "Maybe. Come on, let's go home."

"Damn!" Townsend swore, and dug his heels into his horse's ribs.

Clint took one last look into the grave, where the sun was glinting off something golden and red—precious metal and precious stone?

Maybe, when they got across the border, he'd mention it to Townsend.

Watch for

SON OF A GUNSMITH

211th novel in the exciting GUNSMITH series
from Jove

Coming in August!